The Sister

ERICA KELLY TRAN

DEDICATION

For my family, especially my parents, who transcribed my first stories for me before I was able to write.

For each of my encouraging teachers who requested a copy of my first book so many years ago.

CONTENTS

PROLOGUE

Looking back, I suppose I should have realized that everything had been too easy. There was simply no way the universe could allow it to continue.

Unlike most freshmen, I had assimilated comfortably into my freshman year of high school because of my big brother, Aaron. It was thanks to him that I enjoyed my favorable position at the semi-popular kids' table from the very first day. Of course, given our family's modest, single-parent income, we could never rise to full popularity (according to the unspoken rules), but Aaron's easy going personality, kindness, and sense of humor made him well-liked, both in and out of school. I considered myself extremely fortunate to have even half his social skills, and what's more, his reputation rubbed off on me. I was familiar with his friends, and being known and liked by the seniors trickled down to my own grade, which helped me build my own likable reputation. It seemed like everyone in the school, students and teachers alike, recognized me immediately as

Aaron's sister: we had the same dark, shiny hair, the same shape of hazel eyes, the same splash of freckles across our round faces. He was just a little short for his age; I had just hit my growth spurt. We were practically twins born three years apart.

Aaron was the perfect big brother to me. On the first day of high school, he insisted on driving me in his little green, secondhand Honda Civic, which he sarcastically called The Hulk. He didn't care that he was a senior with a freshman shadow; he was eager to take me, even though Mom was all teary-eyed at the door, sappy and half-crying about how she had wanted to drive her two children on their first day.

He made sure I found my way to homeroom but kept a respectful distance, my personal and self-trained bodyguard. He wouldn't let me sit with him during lunch, claiming I had to make my own friends, but he did introduce me to a few of his friends' siblings. We hit it off as well as any freshmen kids could do on the first day, and within time, we formed a hearty little group. I soon found my own easy stride, but he still kept an eye out for me. I couldn't have been prouder of my big brother or happier with my life. I was aware of how awful high school was supposed to be, having seen the movies and TV shows, and I was relieved to escape the fate of eating lunch alone in a bathroom stall.

A quarter of the school year had passed, nine weeks' worth of good grades and long laughs. Homecoming was a little late in the semester, and the whole school was buzzing in anticipation for the game. The air had just started to taste crisp and clean, and the leaves were preparing for their annual pageantry, though in Louisiana, we weren't treated to many colors. The seniors were especially antsy, with talk of an enormous after-party brewing. Aaron was going; I was not—mandated not by my mother but by Aaron. It was rare that his protectiveness annoyed me, but I knew I would at least get an epic enough account of the party from him to pretend that I had been there in person. Right before we were about to leave for the game, he knocked once on my door and stuck his head in my room.

"Cara?"

"Yeah?"

"Care, check this out," he said. He almost always dropped off the last letter of my name, flicking it carelessly but lovingly away in familiarity. "Look what I got."

I had been doing my makeup, trying to look older than fourteen. "What's up?"

"This was half-price," he said, holding up a bright-blue Spandex unitard against his body, displaying it as proudly as if he'd made it himself. The fabric caught the light, oddly shiny and unnatural. "I'm going to wear it to the game tonight."

"No way," I said, giggling uncontrollably. "You're really going to wear that?"

"Hell yeah." His energy and enthusiasm were absolutely contagious, viral. I stood up and reached for the fabric, stretching it, pulling the endless blue and releasing it.

"I thought you were doing body paint with the guys?" I questioned, rolling my eyeliner pencil between my fingers. He had previously shown me bottles of blue and white paint with just as much excitement. The plan had been to douse himself cerulean with a white letter L emblazoned on his chest. He and his friends were going to spell out the name of our school mascot, the Wolves. Wolves weren't exactly a prevalent threat in central Louisiana, blue wolves even less so. Our mascot was something of a joke amongst the other schools: we attended Greenwood Academy, but our school colors were blue and white. The Greenwood Blue Wolves. Stupid.

"Yeah, but you remember that guy I introduced you to? Tony? He's a junior," Aaron prompted. I tried to picture Tony's face, not following where Aaron was going. "He transferred this year; I'm sure you know him. He still doesn't really have too many friends, so I've been inviting him to hang out with our group. I asked him to come to homecoming with us, and he wanted to do body paint, too, but we already have enough guys to do all the letters. So he was gonna be an exclamation mark, but, I mean…"

I caught on, finally seeing Aaron's intentions. No one wants to be the exclamation mark. It was the leftover, the extra, the pity person. "So you're gonna give up your spot as the L…"

"Yeah. I mean, why not? Who really wants to be the exclamation mark? And he really wanted to be part of it. So I thought I might trade with him, since I don't care that much. Then I figured, I might as well do something crazy, since it's my senior year and all. So I went to the store, and found this, and it was half off, so I'm gonna be the crazy unitard guy."

"That's awesome," I said admiringly, referring to both the unitard and Aaron's kindness.

"Right?" he said, oblivious to his own character. "Care, let me paint your face for you. It'd be so cool."

"No," I said firmly, turning back to my mirror. "I'm just gonna do that warpaint stuff on my cheeks."

"It's called eye black," Aaron said, ever knowledgeable. "You can wear that to any football game. It's homecoming, Care! Come on, let me paint your face blue. With white polka dots. I've already got the paint."

I eyed his unitard. "You're really going to wear that out?"

Aaron's face split into an enormous grin, like he was in danger of losing his jaw. "Let me go text Tony and tell him that he can be the letter L, and then I'll go get the paint. I'll be right back." He dashed out of my room.

"I'm not letting you paint my face!" I called after him, knowing full well that I would.

Later that night, after the popcorn boxes and spilled, sticky drinks and forgotten water bottles were the only things populating the empty bleachers, Aaron dropped me off at home before heading to the party.

"Have fun," I told him before he drove off. "See you later."

How was I to know that the last thing I would say to my brother would be a lie?

CHAPTER 1

"Audie Wells' office calling for Cara Carson."

I rested my forehead against the curve of the steering wheel, holding my phone against my cheek. "This is Cara."

"Hi, Cara. We're just making sure you're still coming to your appointment today."

"Yes," I said. My affirmative hung loosely by itself, unconvincing. "Yes, I'll be there."

"We have your appointment scheduled to have started fifteen minutes ago." The secretary's voice didn't sound accusatory, but guilt bubbled gently in my stomach anyway. I had been various degrees of late to almost every single one of my appointments for the last three years.

"I'm sorry. I'm almost there."

"Alright. See you soon."

The line went silent. I stuffed my phone into my bag on the passenger's seat, then sat up and looked at the dull brick building before me. Not only had I actually been on time for my appointment, I had been ten minutes early. I just couldn't convince myself to leave my car and trudge the long halls to my therapist's office. Again.

I granted myself sixty more seconds of solitude before grabbing my bag and opening my car door to the summer sunshine. To say that it was hot would be an egregious understatement: summer in the south was always heavy with humidity and made even the shortest walks feel like trips through hell. Not that I would actually compare therapy to hell. It wasn't really that bad. I certainly didn't dislike my therapist. Exceptionally kind-hearted, Ms. Wells never pushed or pulled. She listened and made suggestions and listened some more, and when I didn't want to talk, we often sat in comfortable silence. But after not moving forward, or in any direction, really, for the past three years, I probably could have benefited from some pushing and pulling. I wasn't so blind or stupid as to be unable to admit that I was, quite simply, stuck. Stagnant.

From the parking lot, I let the blessedly cool air of the office building carry me to the elevator, up four floors, and down a carpeted corridor to a solid wooden door, 402. I hesitated outside, absentmindedly tracing the golden *A* on the *Audie Wells* placard before sighing. With an effort, I pushed open the door and stepped inside.

"There you are," smiled the secretary as I finally made my way to her little window. Three years, and I still didn't know her name. She handed me the sign-in clipboard, on which I scribbled my name and my long-past appointment time. "You can go right in."

I nodded mutely, hoisted my bag up on my shoulder, and entered Ms. Wells' office, pulling the door closed behind me. She was sitting at her desk in the corner but looked up as I entered, a wide and gracious grin spreading across her face. The fact that Audie Wells smiled, without fail, like she was genuinely happy to see me at each appointment always made me feel better and worse at the same time. I both anticipated and dreaded that smile. At nearly every appointment I had with her, she had always kept her fair hair swept back in an effortless bun, always wrapped herself in a light cardigan, and never wore anything higher than a kitten heel. And even though it occasionally wavered during the course of our talks as she expressed concern or made a point, I knew she would inevitably finish our appointment with that same compassionate smile.

"Hello, Cara," she said, moving from behind her desk to a little armchair in the middle of the room.

"Hi, Ms. Wells," I said, going straight to the worn couch across from her. The office was somewhat dimly lit, with several lamps rather than overhead lighting; a low bookshelf ran along the wall behind her desk. I had been so disappointed on my first visit to see they were all textbooks instead of novels— hard drugs to a desperate escapist like myself. But over time, I had become familiar with the various spines, backbones that bore titles relating to art therapy, music therapy, and other similar techniques. I wouldn't have minded reading one or two of them.

"I'd like to talk with you about your upcoming graduation," Ms. Wells started. I shrugged and casually slid my hand into my purse.

"Go ahead, take it out," she said, gracing me with another gentle smile. *It* was a small crutch of mine that I had the habit of holding onto when I was feeling... anything. Nothing more than a small penny with a star shape stamped out of the middle and a thin leather band threaded through the hole, it had been Aaron's lucky keychain. On some days, Ms. Wells asked me to put it away, to make it through a tough talk without its help. On other days, she granted me permission to clutch at it, as I so often did.

Some days were better than others. Mom sent me to Ms. Wells when I had too many "other" days in a row. But how could I help it? My best friend, my big brother, had been taken from me, in a freak accident of which no one could make sense. He had been driving Letter L Tony back to his house from the party, unfamiliar with the area, and according to witnesses, never even saw the other car coming. And just like that, Aaron was gone. No final goodbyes, no touching hospital scenes. Just gone. I barely spoke for an entire month after it happened. Mom brought me to Ms. Wells in desperation, and even though I wasn't sure if she was helping, I didn't care enough to stop going. Logically, I knew that I didn't actually have to keep coming to these appointments that Mom was forever making for me, but the weird truth was that it seemed like it would take more effort to refuse than to just keep showing up.

When I still didn't answer about graduation, even with keychain in hand, Ms. Wells spoke again. "Would I be wrong in saying that you might be experiencing a little bit of guilt about graduation?"

"You would not be incorrect in saying that," I mumbled.

"Why?"

"Because," I said, then steeled myself. I knew she already knew what I was thinking, but she liked to have me say things out loud. "Aaron never got to go to his. He never got to graduate."

"Would you like to talk more about that?"

"No."

"Alright. What do you expect of your graduation ceremony?"

"My diploma."

"Let me rephrase that. What do you think the ceremony will be like? Let's talk about what you think you might feel." Ms. Wells held her hand out, as if inviting me forward to dance.

I had actually given this a fair bit of thought. "They'll call my name. I'll walk across the stage, take my diploma, shake some hands, flip my tassel. But I think it will sound awkward."

"What will sound awkward?"

I clapped my hands together a few times, demonstrating. "The applause. Either people will clap for me extra loudly because they'll be sympathetic. They'll remember me as the dead boy's sister. Or people will do the stupid slow clap, because they'll be uncomfortable, because I'm the dead boy's sister. No matter what, I won't be Cara. They might as well call out Aaron Carson's Sister, Suma Cum Laude."

Ms. Wells made a small note. "How do you think you'll handle that?"

"I don't know," I shrugged. "I don't even know if that's what will actually happen. Maybe no one will clap at all. Maybe I'll get the exact same applause as everyone else. I really don't want to think about it right now."

Ms. Wells tapped her pen against the file folder that contained all of my information, eyeing me thoughtfully. "Would you prefer to talk about graduation after it's actually happened? I'd love to prepare you for it beforehand, but it seems to me you'd rather not discuss it now."

"Yeah. I'd prefer that."

"We're not putting it off forever," Ms. Wells warned. "Just until your next appointment. I'm confident you'll be able to make it through the actual ceremony."

"Because of my incredible ability to remove myself from a situation instead of staying present," I recited. Ms. Wells was really into being present but marked my inability to do so as one of the shortcomings that held me back.

The corner of Ms. Wells' mouth quirked upwards. "Yes, because of that, though you know I wish you'd stay present through it. It's the mental bullying that you do to yourself after something that worries me."

"Mm."

"I also think it wouldn't be a bad idea if you took your keychain with you," she said. "A little memory to carry with you. To give you something to ground yourself, so that you don't disappear inside your head completely."

I didn't answer.

"But we'll talk about it more next time."

"Are we done today?" I asked hopefully. No matter how late I was, my appointments still had to end at their original time. Ms. Wells had a lot of patients, all around my age, and she liked to keep to her schedule within reason.

"One more thing," she said. I pressed the penny on the keychain against my thumb. "Lots of people find graduation to be sad, after all the confetti has disappeared. It marks the end of an era. You might find yourself dealing with double stress: the normal feelings of confusion as you leave high school behind, and this sense of guilt you have because of your particular situation."

I shrugged to acknowledge that I was listening but not necessarily agreeing.

"I'd like you to think about journaling again."

"I tried that before," I said quickly. "You gave me a notebook. I don't think I wrote even a single sentence."

"I recall. And I didn't press you after I suggested it. You were extraordinarily devoted to your schoolwork, and I didn't want to distract you too much from that."

Another shrug of acknowledgement.

"Why not try again? You're going to have a lot of free time coming up. If you're stuck and don't feel present because you're thinking of him, or whatever situation is troubling you, or you just feel bad— write it out. Put it on paper. And then move on, and be present in the moment," Ms. Wells said.

"I'd rather not."

"Try it anyway. Get it out of your head and onto the paper and let it stay there. Make the commitment that once you write it down, you stop reliving it in your head."

"That's so vague," I argued. "I don't see how that's something I can commit to. We can't always control where our thoughts go. That sounds like I'd have to be tethered to a notebook. I'm not that intense about writing."

Ms. Wells pulled a stack of papers from my files. "Your mom sent me a copy of your senior portfolio. I read through your essays. You're a superb writer."

I should have thanked her for the compliment, but I didn't.

"My concern is that you've been coming here for three years, but truthfully, I'm not seeing as much progress as I would like. I need you to make more of an effort." She said this so gently and with so much care that I felt a tug at my heart. "Graduation represents a large turning point, and I'd like to see you move forward. Let's give writing therapy one more try. Can you make this commitment, Cara?"

My voice felt thick, a cork in my throat around which I could barely talk. "I'm sorry."

"I'm not looking for an apology, Cara," Ms. Wells said. "I'm looking for the best life possible for you. Help me get you there. You've told me you don't want medication. I also know you don't want to stay stuck. Let's keep working on being present and see where that takes us."

"Okay."

Ms. Wells stood up and went to her desk in the corner, where she pulled open a drawer and took out three notebooks. "I'll assume that you cheerfully lost the last notebook I gave you. Red, green, or blue?"

"I don't care."

She walked back and handed me the green notebook, the cheap kind found at the dollar store. I imagined she kept a whole stash in her desk for these kinds of moments. "Green for go."

I flipped it open, took stock of the wafer-thin paper and flimsy cover. It was the exact shade of perfect green that they tell you is a single color in kindergarten, after which it takes you years to unlearn and realize how many different shades and hues and variations there are behind that one name. I distinctly remembered a trip to the beach when I was in middle school, looking out at the ocean and realizing it wasn't blue, but glaucous, ochre, even cesious. Ugly words, beautiful colors.

"Come back, Cara," Ms. Wells sang. I glanced up at her. "Stay present. What were you thinking about?"

"Names of colors," I answered truthfully.

"Yes, I think writing therapy will do you some good, if you can stay focused." Her smile crept back onto her face. "Thank you for coming today."

"Sure," I said, stuffing the notebook and keychain into my bag and standing, recognizing that it was, thankfully, time to go.

"See you next time. Happy graduation."

"Thank you," I said, walking to the door. Ms. Wells went back to her desk, where I knew she would start scribbling notes about our session. "Bye."

"Remember to set up an appointment for after graduation," she called to my back.

"I will," I said, walking out and glancing at the secretary's desk.

I didn't.

CHAPTER 2

This journal is stupid. If Ms. Wells really wants me to use it to stay present, I'd have to hide it under my robes at graduation and write in it during the whole ceremony. And then I'd be distracted by writing and wouldn't pay attention to what's going on. How is that helpful? How is that being any more present?

But if I'm honest with myself, I'd much rather write in here than graduate. Walking across that stage is probably only going to take twenty steps, but it's a walk that will take me that much further away from Aaron. Once I cross it, I can't go back. Graduation is going to be a nightmare.

Graduation, as it turned out, registered as little more than a buzz in my ears and an ache in my neck. I strained my eyes to focus on whoever was speaking on stage instead of on the swinging blue and white tassel in my peripheral vision. I was unexpectedly nervous about stumbling. Ms. Wells' voice thumped along with my heart, rushed along in my veins with my blood: *Stay present, stay present, stay present.* Part of me knew that I was supposed to pay attention to the words of wisdom spilling from the mouths of the speakers. Maybe they could help. Maybe one or two words might actually mean something to me, might find one of the empty, hollow spaces in my brain and nestle down to make a home. But the harder I tried to listen, the fuzzier the words became, and I couldn't understand them.

About halfway through, I gave up trying and checked out. I didn't have any pockets in my graduation robes, so I looped Aaron's keychain around my finger and held onto it like an anchor, but it didn't do much to ground me. I only knew it was my turn to traverse the stage when a teacher at the end of our row ushered all of us out and under the spotlight.

Smatterings of applause waxed and waned as I made my trip with careful steps. I tried to harvest some sort of emotion to attach to the moment, but I couldn't. *Sorry, Ms. Wells.* I briefly wondered if my parents were sitting together but didn't raise my eyes to the audience to check. Instead, I looked out at the sea of blue robes and mortarboards, a mass of blank faces, and pushed away anything that could turn into a thought.

My classmates filed outside after the ceremony came to a close. I let myself be washed out with them, a salmon who had given up trying to swim upstream. Someone led us in our school's fight song, and soon enough, everyone threw their heads back and started howling like wolves. I, too, dropped my head back, staring into the bright sky, just a few shades deeper than the creamy pastel blue of our robes.

"Three... two... one!" A piercing voice cried out, and before I realized what I was supposed to do, the graduates had tossed their mortar boards up into the air. The caps rained back down, comically enormous drops of dry rain, as if they were in a cartoon with an artist who forgot the classic shapes of droplets. Some girls around me scrambled to pick their own caps back up. I stared at the grinning, careless faces, mouths open and moving, hair curled and sprayed and pinned back, choking ties being loosened beneath collars. I pulled my own mortarboard off my head, carefully removed the tassel, then flung the cap as hard and as high as I could, straight up. I watched it pinwheel upwards, but before it could start its descent, I shouldered my way through the crowd and broke into a run, trying not to knee and elbow my peers. It was just windy enough to hold on to the childish, irrational hope that a breeze had caught my cap and carried it off, to a place beyond my limited reality, where someone who had never experienced his own graduation could catch it for me.

"Do you want to frame your tassel?" my mother asked, standing in the doorway of my bedroom and looking at me with a little smile. After graduation, after I had hugged and kissed my father and grandparents, she had left me alone for the whole car ride home and let me be in my room for a while, but it seemed my period of solitude was over.

I tossed the tassel onto the floor and sat up on my bed. "Nope."

"I wish you hadn't lost your cap," Mom said. She took a step into my room. "We could have made a really nice piece of art for your wall."

Without moving my head, I cast a quick glance over the bare, cream-colored walls of my bedroom. A cork bulletin board hung on the wall above my desk. The only thing tacked to it was my final report card, straight A's, with a sticky note from my mother, her neat cursive declaring *I'm so proud of you!* Mom was the only one who ever pinned anything on that board. At one point, it had been covered in mementos and movie tickets and pictures from my freshman year, but after Aaron left, I threw it all away. Whenever Mom put something up, I always took it down, but she never got the hint. She always tacked up something new.

The other walls had a few holes in them where I used to have posters pinned up, not bands or actors or anything, but funky-colored, weird scenes, like dolphins with sunglasses and tie-dye butterflies. Those came down, too. Next to my bed was a calendar still showing October of three years ago. I had told Mom countless times that I just really liked the picture for that month—a cute puppy with a black-and-orange Halloween bow around his neck—but we both knew I couldn't bear to turn the page away from when Aaron had left. How could I move forward in time when he couldn't?

The only thing that indicated I had any personality left was a last picture of myself and Aaron from that fateful homecoming night, blue clad and blue faced, which I either turned to face me or face the wall, depending on my mood. And, of course, my books, stacked into piles that overflowed like waterfalls onto the floor. My beauties, my hideaways, my only remaining friends.

I finally looked at Mom and let the set of my eyebrows speak for me.

Mom sighed, stepping back out of my desolate-looking room and into the hallway. "Alright, Cara. Well, congratulations, again. I'm so proud of you, and I love you very much. Let me know if you want anything special for dinner." She paused. "We can go out if you want."

I inclined my head to let her know I heard, but made no move to get up or follow her downstairs. I flopped back down on my bed. I desperately wanted to go out to eat, not for myself, but for her, under the pretense of how a normal family would celebrate such a happy occasion as graduation. But even my mother's happiness didn't seem worth the effort. I curled in on myself in disgust. The thought of going out and seeing other families celebrating, seeing other families full and whole, complete, doing something as simple as enjoying a meal, took my appetite away. But that wasn't fair to Mom.

With an enormous effort, I lifted my head off my pillow and tried to make my voice carry through the hall, down the stairs, and into the living room, where Mom was no doubt going through graduation pictures on her phone of me with my tight-lipped smile.

"Mom?"

The stairs creaked as her footsteps rushed up them. Her head appeared at the top of the landing. "Sweetie?"

"Maybe we could..." I wet my lips and pushed the words out past my teeth. "Order Chinese, have it delivered, or something? For my graduation dinner?"

Her eyes lit up at my request. "Is that what you want? That sounds delicious. Let me go get the takeout menus. Or do you already know what you want?"

"Um. Chicken lo mein. And fried rice."

"Of course," Mom said brightly, then hesitated. "I got you a cake, too, so we can have that for dessert. Ice cream cake."

"Mom," I protested. She sighed.

"I just want to celebrate this special occasion with you, Cara. And cake seems like a good way to do it. Alright?"

"Alright," I relented. She beamed, then dashed downstairs again. I sat there, picking at a loose thread in my shabby quilt. The summer before my freshman year, Mom promised I could have a new comforter set in whatever design I wanted, to celebrate my transition to high school. Aaron had gotten a new desk when he was a freshman. I was thrilled at the idea of replacing my childhood bedding and spent weeks pouring over catalogs. But I never got around to picking one, and by the time Mom hesitatingly brought it up again, Aaron had already left us, and the idea of more change made me crumple and cling to the threadbare quilt I already had. My bright green notebook from Ms. Wells looked ludicrous against the patchwork of muted colors. I nudged it off the bed with my foot.

When I heard the doorbell ring, a tinny tune announcing the arrival of our food, I made my way downstairs to find the kitchen transformed. Mom had turned off the lights and lit all kinds of candles, tea lights and tall tapers, wax-clumped stubs and aromatherapy rounds with multiple wicks, and placed them along the table. Our kitchen seemed transfigured from its usual pedestrian familiarity to a new and mysterious setting, the table like a secluded booth in an intimate restaurant. We ate by the flickering light, our shadows joining our party. Mom's face, lit from beneath, looked like she was glowing from within, making her smile seem even brighter. She must have pulled out every candle we had in the entire house. I forked rice into my mouth and chased long noodles with clumsy chopsticks, trying not to let any of my movements extinguish the candles at my elbows. Our conversation was sparse, but Mom didn't seem to mind.

She pulled the cake out of the freezer when we had finished dinner, setting it before me. I tried to remember the Cara who had loved chocolate chip ice cream, who would add chunks of baking chocolate to any flavor ice cream just to satisfy her sweet tooth. But this cake just seemed like another chore to complete.

"Blow out the candles!" Mom chirped gleefully, clasping her hands and smiling at me.

"It's not my birthday," I said stubbornly.

"Humor me, Cara," said Mom. I looked down at the table, quickly counting the thirteen candles in their dishes and stands.

"Unlucky," I commented.

"Thirteen years in school," she explained. "Kindergarten through twelfth grade." I realized that she would never have another graduation to celebrate, with me or with anyone else. This was it. Thirteen years of schooling and suddenly done forever, considering I wasn't going to college.

"One try," I conceded. "I'm not going to attempt to get them all."

"Fine, fine," she said quickly. I blew out a stream of air through my mouth, turning my head in a small arc. The five flames closest to me trembled and vanished.

"Almost half!" Mom clapped, undeterred. She paused, as if waiting for me to blow out the rest, then bent over the table and blew them out herself. Smoke curled lazily upwards, stretching, reaching, disappearing. I followed the individual wisps with my eyes until they dissipated above my head.

"And now the cake," she said, and then started hacking away at the ice cream cake with a knife. "Shoot. Cake's still frozen. I should have taken it out earlier."

"It's alright," I said. "We can eat it later."

Mom sighed and dropped the knife on the counter with a clatter. "Sorry, sweetie."

"Really, Mom," I said. "It's not a big deal." Silence grew in the absence of cake. I dropped my gaze to the crumpled, greasy takeout bags and empty containers, rice still stuck to the sides. Mom plopped back into her chair, looking as defeated as the bags.

"C'mon, Mom. Have a fortune cookie," I said, sliding one across the table towards her. She smiled, crinkling the plastic wrapper in her fingers, then glanced pointedly at the other one. I rolled my eyes but grinned, then tore open the wrapping and crunched the cookie into pieces. Mom snapped hers crisply in half.

"Hm," she said, popping a piece into her mouth and mumbling around the cookie. "Let's see. My fortune says, *Be productive in your work, and productivity will follow.*"

"That's basically a null sentence," I laughed. Mom chuckled.

"What's yours say?"

I unfurled the little strip of paper previously trapped inside my cookie, turned it over, turned it over again.

It was blank.

"Bad omen," I joked.

"Or a good one," Mom countered.

"Or just null, like yours."

We both laughed, a light feeling floating in my chest that hadn't existed in months. I had to admit, it was nice to spend an evening with Mom; it was nice to laugh. If I concentrated, I could almost taste a hint of normalcy. But after we had finally sawed through the frozen cake and I retreated back to my room, I tacked the blank fortune to my bulletin board. It stared at me, faceless, speechless. I smiled grimly back at it. Its emptiness affirmed my own.

CHAPTER 3

No updates. No progress. Lots of Aaron thoughts. Would we have gone to the same college? Would he be helping me get ready? Giving me notes from classes he took? What would he have majored in? What would I be majoring in if I weren't so stupid? I can't believe I'm not going to college. I can't believe how much I messed this up.

Summer loomed before me, deep and seemingly endless, as blank as my little fortune. I could not settle on a particular emotion to express my feelings towards graduation, but at least I had accessible emotions from which to choose. On the one hand, I was grateful to be free of the cold halls swarming with teenage hormones, free of the unforgiving fluorescent lights, free of the crappy food and lonely lunches that I had managed to avoid for that first perfect quarter of freshman year. But on the other hand, school was no longer the beautiful and much needed distraction to which I had grown all but addicted. I knew my fellow graduates were sleeping off the past thirteen years of early mornings, finding themselves renewed and energized with the summer sun. I could not share in their enjoyment. I waged a constant battle against myself, a civil war with one soldier from, on, and against both sides.

Before, I had enjoyed school for its social purposes, and, being naturally bright, enjoyed most of my classes and spent time with my friends. But it wasn't until after Aaron passed away that I began to recognize school as a safe haven of pure escapism. I relished the chance to sit in a room where someone demanded that I think about what they were teaching, that and only that. All I had to do was listen and hold onto whatever I heard. It wasn't that I got to turn my brain off, per se, but that I got to focus all of my attention and energy on something so far removed from me. I craved the classroom, studied long into the night, and poured facts and figures into my head as quickly as I could. I cherished the opportunity of being held accountable for something. Without accountability, I had little reason to keep moving. I couldn't find comfort in any of my old friends, who had no idea what to say to me. I blocked all their attempts at empathy and pushed them away. I sought solace only through the fictional characters of books and the steady concentration of school. School was my sanctuary.

And then, my mistake. In a fit of apathy, I told the school guidance counselor that I would not be attending college. I still cannot say what possessed me to do so. She had a long, serious talk with me about how it's true that college isn't for everyone, but she *believes in me*, and tried to bargain by getting me to just apply to the local community college. I accepted the application but threw it away the next day, ignoring her due date reminders and phone calls. My poor mother went back and forth between the two of us, worrying for my future but afraid of driving me away. I secretly suspected that she didn't push me too hard towards college because she was afraid of a completely empty house. Our house already seemed to echo without Aaron.

I realized my mistake the second after final exams had finished. The bell rang, the seniors cheered, and my heart dropped into my stomach as I walked out of the building for the last time. I had actually denied myself the best escape from the grief of losing Aaron that I had ever found. What an idiot. Even if I were to apply to a college in the future, there would be no reason for them to accept me, on account of my sheer stupidity.

Mom finally decided two weeks into the summer that my moping about was more intense than my usual brooding. "Cara, sweetie. Isn't there anything you want to do?"

"No," I said flatly from my sprawled out position on the couch. My arms ached from holding a book above my face to read. "This is exciting. This is absolutely the life. I love this nothingness." I sat up and closed my book, giving Mom a sarcastic little smile to let her know I wasn't a complete nihilist.

She sat down next to me and patted my leg. "I just want you to be happy, Cara. I want you to find some sort of happiness."

"I'm not unhappy," I argued.

"Well, I hate to say it, Cara, but you haven't done much over these past two weeks."

"Mom. I'm not going to figure out what to do with my

life overnight."

"I know," she said earnestly. "But it's been fourteen overnights. And many nights before then, sweetie. You see what I'm saying?"

I knew what she was saying. I had been listless and drifting, not just for the past two weeks, but for the past three years. I wanted to respond, but there was nothing new for me to say. I stared at my book.

"I set up another appointment for you with Audie," Mom said. "With Ms. Wells. This Thursday, nine in the morning. Okay?"

"What?" I said sharply. "Mom, I just went! I seriously just saw her, right before graduation."

"I know," Mom said gently. "And her secretary called me after that to say you hadn't set up your next appointment like Ms. Wells asked. I think you need a little more guidance right now. I think it would be good for you. What harm could it do?"

She waited for me to argue, but I didn't say anything. The knowledge sat, heavy in the pit of my stomach, that this summer would not come to an end. This summer would stretch on into fall and winter and the rest of my life if I didn't do something. I turned my book over in my hands a couple of times before finally looking at Mom. Sitting with Ms. Wells for an hour probably wouldn't solve anything, but maybe she might be able to find a speck of hope for me.

"Okay. Thursday at nine. I'll be there." I knew I had overreacted. Mom making the appointment herself hadn't been much of a surprise anyway. She always called and set them up— she worked as a receptionist in a dentist's office and was always on top of scheduling.

She leaned over and kissed my cheek. "I think it will be worth it, Cara."

"Let's hope so," I mumbled, unconvinced. Mom patted my leg one more time, then stood and left the room. I exhaled deeply and tried to find my place in my book, a much easier task than finding my place in the world.

"Hi, Cara," Ms. Wells said brightly from her desk as I entered her office, only eight minutes late this time, closing the door to the waiting room behind me. The glow from her computer screen lit her face; she clicked a couple of times with her mouse, then stood. "Congratulations on your graduation!"

"Thank you," I replied. We both took our usual seats.

"So!" Ms. Wells said, smiling at me. I waited. "How was the ceremony?"

"Long. And boring."

"I can understand that. Did you at least have a good commencement speaker?"

"Just our valedictorian spoke. And the principal, I think," I said, not answering her question directly, as I couldn't remember either of their speeches.

"Well, for all its boringness, it's a nice little rite of passage," Ms. Wells said. She flipped a page in her notebook and put her pen to the paper without taking her eyes off me. "And I'm so proud of you, both for completing your high school career and attending your graduation. You didn't *have* to do either, but you made choices and decisions, and look how far you've come."

She paused and waited for me to speak, but I just shrugged. I didn't feel like I'd come very far at all.

"Was it as difficult to sit through as you thought it would be?" she asked after a moment. "Not just because it was boring, but because of Aaron?"

"I held his keychain," I said, dancing around her question again. "Didn't have any pockets."

"Can you tell me five things about your graduation?"

"To prove that I was mentally present? Sure. One, we sang our alma mater and our fight song. Two, both of my parents attended, although I don't know if they actually sat together or not. Three, the girl sitting next to me had way too much perfume on. Three and a half, the guy behind me had way too much cologne on. Four..." I faltered. I should have saved the cologne comment for its own number. "Um, four, I tossed my cap with my classmates, but I lost it. And five... my mom and I celebrated with Chinese food after."

"Good details," Ms. Wells said. "What was the valedictorian's name?"

"I don't know."

"Did they call your middle name when you walked across the stage, or just your first and last?"

I frowned. "I don't remember."

"We'll keep working on being present," she said gently. "Let me ask another question. Were you grateful to be at graduation?"

"No," I admitted. "I didn't want to be there."

"Why not?"

"You know why not. Because of the guilt. Because of Aaron."

"That would have been a perfect opportunity to practice the gratitude exercise we've talked about before," Ms. Wells said. Her tone was not accusing in the slightest, merely commentary; friendly, even. "Whenever you find yourself in situations where you feel guilt over what you've been able to accomplish that Aaron was not, you can honor his life by choosing to be grateful for your experiences."

"I know," I mumbled. "It's just hard to remember in the moment."

The thing about Ms. Wells was that she never made me feel bad about my failures, or my poor attitude, or my silence. I made myself feel bad, with the mental bullying she pointed out in me, but she never acted as if I owed her anything. The comfort in her smile was enough to give me, at times, a brief sense of peace.

She changed the subject for me. "May I ask how your writing has been going?"

"Good," I lied. My two pitiful journal entries hardly qualified as writing. Together, they didn't even take up a whole page.

"Would you like to tell me about it?"

"Ummm…" I chewed my lip. "No. It's private?"

"And that's perfectly fine," Ms. Wells said encouragingly. Her pen had been flying across her paper, but she finally paused in her writing, though she had never looked down. "Now, last time, I asked you to make an appointment before you left, but your mom is the one who usually makes your appointments for you, right?"

"Right."

"And she made this one. Has something happened in the last few weeks? Something that may have prompted her to make the appointment?"

"Ironically," I said conversationally, "nothing has happened in the last few weeks at all. That's the problem."

"I don't understand."

"I'm not going to college, Ms. Wells."

"Yes, I remember talking about that."

I started counting on my fingers. "I just graduated high school. I don't have a summer job. I don't have a life goal. I'm not going to college. I didn't realize... I just don't know what to do without school. Without anything. And I'm... scared."

"Scared?"

"I just don't know what to do."

"Is that something you feel the need to figure out right away?"

"Well, no," I said. "But I need *something* to do. The more I sit around doing nothing, the more I think about Aaron. The more I think about everything. I'm worrying my mom. I need something to focus on."

"I'm pleased to hear you say that." Ms. Wells made another note. "It's good that you can identify that need. Now, you mentioned that you don't have a summer job. Do you feel like that's an option?"

"It's not," I said quickly.

"Why not?"

I sat back a little, staring at her and chewing on my lip, trying to think of how to put my anxiety and restlessness into words for her. How would I ever explain myself on a résumé? *Aimless teen with no work ethic or desire to make personal connections* wouldn't look great in print. "It's just not."

Ms. Wells, thankfully, did not press me on that option, though I fully expected to hear about it in a future session. She looked at me thoughtfully for a minute, then stood up abruptly and went to her desk, pulling open a drawer. For a moment, I thought she was going to whip out another notebook for me, but she only had a handful of papers that looked like fliers and brochures.

"Have you ever thought about volunteering, Cara?" she asked, handing me the papers. "Depending on what organizations you look at, you could find something that would give you a similar structure and concentration level as a job without the, ah, institutional confines, if you will."

I hesitantly thumbed through the first few fliers. Pleas to volunteer at soup kitchens, churches, animal shelters, nursing homes— my stomach flip-flopped.

"Um, I'm not sure if this is what I really should be doing..." I stammered. "I just don't think... I don't feel like it's... the solution. For me. I'm not ready for something this... big."

Ms. Wells' pen stopped, and she looked down at what she had written. I resisted the urge to lean forward and try to read her upside-down writing.

"May I see those papers again?" she asked, holding out her hand. I gave them back. She rifled through them, stopped at one, and extracted it from the stack. Again, she went to her desk and rummaged through the drawers before pulling out a crisp white envelope. She folded the flier, flipped open the flap with her slender fingers, and slipped the single page inside.

"Here," she said, closing the envelope as she walked back over. "Don't open it just yet. Take it home, open it there. Not in front of me, not in front of your mom. Really sit and think about this one, Cara. Visualize yourself there as part of it. If you feel yourself starting to get worked up or anxious, put it back in the envelope, and do something else. If you feel angry, think about why you feel that way, and then try to work through it rationally. And think about it again. Okay? You're not obligated to actually do anything. But I would really appreciate it if you gave this some serious thought."

"Uh, alright," I said, wholly confused. I fumbled with my bag's clasp, trying to stuff the envelope inside without bending it. "Is that all for today?"

"That's all for today," Ms. Wells said, smiling again, all previous gravity gone. "Remember, you have my number, so you can always call me if you want more information. Or just to talk. But I really hope you give this a lot of consideration."

"I will," I said quickly. Ms. Wells stood and walked me to the door of her office.

"Remember, you can make an appointment right here, right now," she said gently. "You don't have to wait and make your mother worry."

"I know," I said, trying to smile. Ms. Wells grinned, patted my shoulder, and then went back into her office and sat down at her desk. I closed the door behind me, glanced at the secretary behind her little window, and strode right past her.

In the lonely privacy between my bare bedroom walls, I sat heavily down on my bed, envelope in hand. I couldn't imagine which organization Ms. Wells thought was so important that she had to send me home to look at it. I pulled out the paper, smoothed it flat against my lap, took a breath, and unfolded it, trying to prepare myself for whatever it said.

Bold, rounded text jumped out at me, childish and silly. A headline roared: SUMMER SIBLINGS. Below, a simply drawn stick-figure duo grinned up at me, one figure much shorter than the other. At the bottom of the page I found bullet points:

- Are you a teenager between the ages of 14-18?
- Did you complete your freshman year?
- Are you fun-loving?
- Do you want to give back to your community?

Then the SUMMER SIBLINGS is the group for you!

Sign up this summer to be paired with an underprivileged child in your community. You will be responsible for attending group-organized events with your assigned sibling and showing them love, fun, and friendship. Must be ENTHUSIASTIC, CARING, and READY TO PLAY! We are committed to giving these children great opportunities, and we are SERIOUS about having FUN!

Contact Earla Jameson for more information.

I folded the flier in half, then unfolded it and read it again. Some strange emotion was building up in me, but I couldn't place it. I crumpled up the flier and threw it across my room, then crumpled up myself, clutching my knees to my body, tucking my chin in. She'd been right.

I could practically hear her voice in my head. *Really sit and think about it, Cara. If you feel yourself starting to get worked up or anxious, put it down and do something else. If you feel angry, think about why you feel that way, and then try to work through it rationally. And think about it again.*

I unfurled myself limb by limb, then dug in my bag and

pulled out my phone, touching the screen and scrolling through my contacts. Aaron's number was the first on the list. My thumb hovered over his name, but I forced it past and landed on *Audie Wells - Office*.

"Cara, hi!" she answered after her secretary had transferred me. "Did you forget something at the office?"

"No," I said. "I was calling to ask you why you gave me the Summer Siblings flier."

There was a pause on her end. "Have you had enough time to think about it?"

"I can't think about it until I know the reasoning behind it," I said, confused. "I just don't understand. Are you—are you trying to replace Aaron?"

I could hear a sort of muffled noise, as if she were switching the phone from one ear to another. "What do you think is the reasoning behind it? Why do you think you're reacting this strongly?"

"I don't know. That's why I called."

"I think this is a wonderful opportunity for you, Cara. It's about putting that love you have for your brother to good use," Ms. Wells said gently. "You have so much sisterly love inside of you. I think the Summer Siblings would be a beautiful way to keep that love alive."

I mulled on that for a minute.

"This is your chance to do something. I know that's scary. Do you have any other questions?"

"Not right now," I said. I felt a little deflated, like I had been gearing up for a fight that went nowhere. As usual, Ms. Wells had nailed my own emotions when I couldn't figure them out for myself. "I, uh… I guess I need to think about it some more."

"Please do," Ms. Wells said. "Please give it a lot of thought. Put it down, walk around. Journal a little. Think some more. You know the drill."

"Okay," I answered. "I will."

"I'm glad you called," she told me. "Have a good afternoon, Cara."

"You too," I said, then hung up.

A light pressure on my forehead startled me awake. I blinked blearily, my eyes focusing on the dim shape before me: my mother, with her hand smoothing back my long hair.

"Cara, sweetie, you've been up here for a while," she said in a low voice. "Don't you want anything to eat?" Judging by the lack of light in my room, I guessed that I had fallen asleep and slept through the day.

Vague hunger echoed in my empty stomach, but I didn't want to get up. "No, I'll just eat a really big breakfast." I closed my eyes.

"Is something wrong, Cara?"

I opened my eyes again. Something was always wrong. Something had been wrong for years. Mom peered down at me, concern written into the lines etched around her drawn mouth. She was in her scrubs: another day behind the desk at the dentist's office. I thought how easy it would be to let my mother make my decisions for me the way she made appointments, for me to spin the story and convince her to call up Audie Wells and get me out of this decision altogether.

"Ms. Wells gave me something big to think about today," I said sleepily, if not a little cryptically.

"Oh?"

"Yeah. I just don't know what to do."

"Do you want me to talk to her?" Mom asked. I could practically see the memorized phone number to the office lighting up behind her eyes.

She looked so tired, standing there over me, ever vigilant and alert to my needs, as if she had to pour all the maternal attention and affection she would have given to her two children into one. I reached out and grabbed her hand, soft and fleshy and cool.

"No," I said, the word heavy but determined. "Thank you, but no." Mom squeezed my hand and bent down to kiss my cheek.

"Alright. I'll see you in the morning," she said. I slunk under my quilt as she left my room, waiting for sleep to reclaim me.

But it never did. I tossed and turned fitfully, crawling out from under the covers when it got hot, snaking back under when I felt too exposed. My brain raced through a hundred different scenarios. I thought of the little orange bottle of prescription sleeping pills in the bathroom vanity, which I was under strict orders to reserve only for the roughest of nights, and only under Mom's supervision. Taking one now, though, would mean that I would sleep through the morning and be in a stupor for the rest of the day, which would mean questioning from Mom, which would mean even more appointments with Ms. Wells. My eyes burned. I let the night laugh at me before it slipped out the window, running from the dawn, the hours rolling away.

With the weak morning light struggling around the window shade, I stared at my ceiling, my dry eyes unfocused as I struggled to capture my thoughts. They floated up and away towards my slowly turning ceiling fan, where they were buffeted about in the air. I watched them bounce off the molding, colliding and bursting into new fragments of thought, none of which seemed to form a solid decision.

They couldn't pair me up with a new big brother—not that I wanted one. But they could pair me up with a "brother," and maybe that would be enough. It had to be enough. I was teetering on the edge. Surely a pseudo-brother would help to keep me from shattering altogether, would keep me from floating away in the dust because there was nothing weighing me down. But would I be able to handle it? Would I collapse under the pressure?

I had heard of bigger, national organizations, similar to the Summer Siblings, but here was a local opportunity, sitting at my feet. It was almost too perfect, and that frightened me. I could be a sister again. It was a terrifying thought disguised behind elation. I could barely stand to think it. I could be a sister again. Maybe it would be enough.

It had to be enough.

CHAPTER 4

This is good. This is good for me. This is action. This is doing. This is what life is supposed to be. This is GOOD.

This is bad, I thought, capping my pen and tucking it alongside my bright green journal in my bag. *I am lying to a notebook.* Writing in it had not relieved the anxiety of waiting, as I had hoped, while I sat in a hard wooden chair in a cold and empty hall. With my decision made, Ms. Wells had directed me to the large government building where the Summer Siblings office resided, where I was now waiting to meet with the organization's director, the Earla Jameson from the flier. I felt a little like a kid waiting outside of the principal's office, but I was trying to convince myself that it was the right place for me to be, despite the lonely gloom of the hallway. Occasionally, a person would click down the hall in high heels or shuffle from room to room, but no one joined me in the waiting game.

A flickering fluorescent light bulb directly over my head threatened to turn into a headache. I closed my eyes and tilted my head back against the wall, trying not to let anxiety overtake me.

"Absolutely. Don't even worry about it for a minute, Mrs. J. I won't be at the planning meeting, but I'll see you later."

The voice sounded close but muffled. I opened my eyes and sat up straighter, straining my ears to hear the conversation happening on the other side of the door.

"Okay. I'll swing by again tomorrow." I jumped as the door slammed open, casting my eyes towards the ceiling and trying to look like I wasn't eavesdropping.

"Well, what d'you know?" said the person. I swung my gaze from the ceiling to his face. "If it isn't Cara Carson!"

"Adam…" I said, caught off-guard, but although I recognized him instantly, no last name swam to my lips. We had gone to both middle and high school together, and though he was an exceptionally friendly person, we had never actually been friends. He used to be on the stockier side but had thinned out a bit during high school, though his face was still round, and always seemed to be laughing at something. What really made him stick out was the distinctive color of his hair: not ginger or auburn or classic red, but a coppery sort of color, like a shiny new penny straight from the mint.

"Adam Beck," he prompted, folding his arms good-naturedly and leaning against the doorframe. "Don't tell me you've forgotten me after just a couple of weeks."

"I didn't forget you," I said. "But it's not like I ever really knew you to begin with."

"Well, I knew you."

"Everyone knew me," I pointed out. "Dead guy's sister."

I purposefully meant to make him feel awkward, to leave me alone, but he only twisted his mouth and shrugged his shoulders, not disagreeing.

"So what brings you all the way out here?" he asked conversationally. "You wouldn't happen to be waiting for a meeting with Mrs. Jameson, would you?"

I stood up irritably. "Why else would I be sitting out in the hall like this?"

Adam flicked a smile at me before calling back into the office. "Mrs. Jameson! You've got a Miss Cara Carson out here waiting to speak with you!"

"May I?" I frowned, gesturing at the door. Adam unglued himself from the doorframe and stepped away, giving me space to move inside.

"Catch you later, Cara," he said, breezing past me and waving. "Have a good day!"

I ignored him and closed the door behind me. The room was small and windowless, lit by the same fluorescent lighting as the hallway. A gorgeously elegant woman was sitting behind the scratched and chipped resin desk in the middle of the room. She seemed larger than life, almost out of place amidst the old office furniture.

"Well, you must be Cara Carson, then," she said. She was as opposite in appearance from Ms. Wells as could be, but exuded the same warmth in her smile. She wore multiple layers of printed fabrics which popped against her dark skin, heavy earrings and bangles, and a bright, effervescent scarf tied around her neck. I couldn't take my eyes off of it. She was such a solid presence, but it was as if she had an impressionist painting at her throat. "I'm Mrs. Jameson."

She extended her hand across the desk. Her bangles

clanked and clacked at her wrist as I shook hands before sitting down in the single empty chair. Mrs. Jameson looked at me with round, expectant, friendly eyes.

"Um, I'm here about the Summer Siblings," I said, feeling my palms begin to sweat.

"I would hope so!" Mrs. Jameson chuckled, a deep, throaty sound that shook her whole body. My insides squirmed a little. I wondered if I should tell her I had been sent by my therapist, or if I should let her think I was normal for as long as I could.

"Well, I, uh, saw your flier—"

"Hold on just one second, dear," Mrs. Jameson said. She shifted in her seat so that she was angled towards her ancient, whirring computer, the screen of which I could not see. Slowly and a little uncertainly, she moved the mouse, clicking with great force at intervals. Silence blossomed around us. I inspected the wall behind her desk, hung with pictures of groups of children and crayon drawings. A bin of worn children's books sat in the corner of the room.

Mrs. Jameson sighed. "Computers!"

"Yeah," I said, not sure how to reply.

"You see, I have an email somewhere on here…" Mrs. Jameson brought her face closer to the screen. "Ah! Yes, here it is. I'd print it out, but I don't have a printer." She chuckled again; I smiled uncertainly. "Audie said you might be coming today."

"Oh, she did?" I asked, feeling a little relieved, a little disappointed.

"Oh, yes. Audie and I are great friends. She occasionally sends helpers my way when she thinks they could benefit from the Summer Siblings," Mrs. Jameson informed me.

"And I keep an eye on all the children and send them to her if I think they could benefit from something more... structured than the SS, you see. She works with youth and adolescents."

"I'm aware," I said dryly.

"I'm deeply sorry for your loss, dear," Mrs. Jameson said suddenly. Her voice resonated with true sympathy.

"Thank you," I said automatically. So she knew.

"So let's have us a little chat about what we do in the Summer Siblings and how you might fit in."

"Alright," I said. I wasn't sure what I had been expecting from this meeting, but I tried to arrange my face so that it looked like I was totally prepared for this conversation.

Mrs. Jameson picked up one of the picture frames on her desk and smiled at it. "I'm sure you've heard about the bigger organizations like us. The national ones. The Summer Siblings started out as a little after-school program with just a couple of kids. You see, dear, I used to be a teacher. I taught third grade. The children are still so loving and lovable at that age, but they can all tie their shoes, you see?"

"Uh huh."

"I worked with a high school teacher who would send her students over to read and play with my younger students after school. It was just something I sort of did on my own, with the permission of the principals of both schools, and the parents, of course. I called it the Schoolyard Siblings. But then I took a sabbatical for my health, and after a lot of consideration, decided to retire from teaching."

"Ah," I murmured. I hoped she didn't expect a rendition of my own life story after hers.

"But I just couldn't let go of this little project of mine. I brought it to the state. It went back and forth for a couple of years. But here we are. I have my own office and everything now," she said, spreading her arms and beaming at the four peeling walls. "You see, I just knew we could do some good if we had the resources. And now we've got them, through the state, you see. But we're more of a summer camp now, state-wide. And I changed the name."

"It's still alliterative," I commented. Mrs. Jameson smiled.

"Well, dear, that's how the official Summer Siblings got started. So let me give you a rundown of what all we do." She bent behind her desk and shuffled through a stack of papers on the ground. "Here you are."

She handed me a flier identical to the one that Ms. Wells had given me. I accepted it without mentioning that I had a copy of it in my purse.

"Adam Beck just stopped by and offered to deliver some of these fliers to local camps for me. Such a considerate young man. You see, sometimes, camp counselors might notice a child who could benefit from the Summer Siblings," Mrs. Jameson told me. "I believe there are lots of children out there who could benefit from our work, but we've got to find them first. We send our fliers to a lot of different places."

I made a monosyllabic sound.

"Do you have any questions so far, dear?"

"Well..." I started. "I'm still not one hundred percent certain about what the Summer Siblings actually *do*. I mean, I sort of get it, but I guess I'd just like to know some details."

"Excellent question!" Mrs. Jameson pronounced. I could hear the teacher in her voice. "Underprivileged children from elementary schools, and occasionally middle schools, are recommended for the program because of their need for a guiding figure in their lives. Older children— although I suppose you aren't really a child, are you— provide that guiding figure. We attend all sorts of activities together and give the children a chance to have fun and escape their situations for a while. These children come from all different backgrounds and have all different reasons for needing a Sibling, do you see?"

"Yes, I see," I said. "And how do you find the older, uh, siblings?"

"Most volunteer because they've seen a flier or heard about it from a teacher or counselor. I make sure that all the schools in our district are aware of it. As I mentioned earlier, people with professions like Audie Wells let me know when they think someone would do well within our group."

"Well, here I am," I said, leaning back in my chair.

"Cara, dear," Mrs. Jameson said, folding her hands and placing them on top of her desk. "We don't see situations such as yours too often."

"Situations such as mine?"

"We like to provide our children with very stable siblings, because that's often the only form of stability that they receive outside of school. My staff does interview each older sibling before pairing them with a younger child, but I'm handling your interview personally because of the reason Audie recommended you. I understand that you're here for part of the healing process on your own end. I just really need to be certain that you are committed to providing that same healing for your assigned sibling."

"Oh. Well, sure. We help each other heal. Ms. Wells likes to say that," I said. She never said anything like it. I figured a little white lie wouldn't hurt. "Ms. Wells thought this would be a good idea. And... I agree. And I'm, uh, stable."

Mrs. Jameson gently pressed her long, polished nails to her puckered lips, staring at me all the while. "We help each other heal. I like that."

I looked away.

"Cara, can you tell me what being a sibling means to you?"

Images of Aaron flooded my mind. I thought of how incredible he would have been at something like this. He would have poured all his time and energy into mentoring a kid. I would have been jealous, but the thing about Aaron was that his love for me wouldn't have decreased in the slightest. It would have grown.

Feeling my eyes fill with tears, I pretend to sneeze to give myself an excuse to wipe at my face. Mrs. Jameson handed me a tissue across her desk and graciously looked away for a moment before repeating her question.

"Um..." I paused for a moment to let my voice steady. "When we were kids... my brother, my brother Aaron, and I, were walking home from school one day. And while we were walking home, he found this penny on the ground, except it had the shape of a star kind of cut or stamped out of the middle. I thought it was pirate treasure or something. He loved it. We had never seen anything like it."

I realized I was tearing the tissue to shreds. I took another breath and continued. "He went to our dad, who helped him make this leather cord for it that they looped through the star cutout to make a kind of keychain. It was his prized possession."

Another breath. I pulled the keychain out of my bag and

showed Mrs. Jameson. "He carried it with him everywhere for a week, and I asked to see it every single day. The next time I asked to see it, he said he couldn't show me, because he had put it in my backpack for me. He gave it to me. Just like that, it was mine. He didn't think twice about it. We wound up trading it back and forth every other month, sharing it equally, for— for the rest of his life."

Mrs. Jameson looked at me with shining eyes.

"I guess that's what I think being a sibling means. I mean, there's fighting and arguing and stuff, but it's mostly sharing and loving each other. Obviously, Aaron was the best there ever was, but... he was a great example." I swallowed hard. Mrs. Jameson let a moment pass.

"Can you promise me, dear, that you will put your full effort into being a big sister to your little sibling?" she finally asked me.

"Yes," I said quickly and forcefully, perhaps a little too much so. "I promise."

"Well then," Mrs. Jameson said, smiling widely. "I think that after you've filled out the necessary forms, and we've signed all the right papers in the right spots, that you will be a very welcomed new member of the Summer Siblings."

"Really? Just like that?"

"I'll take care of most everything, dear," Mrs. Jameson assured me. "We just need your standard information. We'll also run a little background check; nothing to be alarmed about. It's just what we have to do. If everything checks out, and I'm sure it will, I'll pair you up with a sibling right away. I already have someone in mind."

"Thank you, Mrs. Jameson," I said, a little surprised at how easy this was going to be. Just a few forms away from having a surrogate little brother.

"You know, we're having a meeting next Thursday," Mrs. Jameson said, glancing at a calendar tacked onto the wall. "I would love to see you there, so you could meet some of your peers in the group."

"Peers?" My heart rate picked up. I hadn't expected to work with anyone my own age in any sort of social setting. "Uh, do you think my forms will be through in time for next week?"

"I'll personally make sure of it," Mrs. Jameson winked at me amicably. "Cara, dear, thank you so much for your interest in our little program. We help each other heal. Oh, I like that very much. I'll have to ask Audie if she made that up or if she's quoting someone."

"Of course," I said, fumbling for the straps of my bag. My legs felt somewhat numb, but I managed to stand. "I, um, I'll see you later, Mrs. Jameson."

"Goodbye, dear."

After Aaron's death, I refused to drink coffee. It kept me awake and jittery. The few times I had forced it down, my mind, a hyperactive hamster on a wheel, had raced through a hundred topics that I would have preferred to avoid. I was always happy to have my mind occupied, but when caffeinated, I couldn't control it. And that was why I had awkwardly ordered a bottle of water from the girl behind the counter at the coffee shop where the Summer Siblings meeting was taking place. Mom had dragged every last detail out of me about the interview with Mrs. Jameson, and when she heard there was a group meeting, she had insisted that I attend, driving me here herself. Which is how I wound up being early for once.

At the moment, I was sitting uncomfortably in a wobbly chair, clutching my water bottle, trying to people-watch to take my mind off of the meeting. Unfortunately for me, there weren't too many people to watch. My skin started crawling with nerves, little worry-worms that burrowed in my veins.

"Oh, my God, Cara?" I heard someone say against a backdrop of tinkling bells. I turned around in my seat to see a tall, thin girl standing in the doorway of the coffee shop. I shielded my eyes against the sun behind her.

"That's totally you! How've you been?" she squealed. Julie Singer. One of the girls in the group of friends from which I had drifted away after Aaron's death. I hoped she wouldn't want to hug me. Julie's blonde-streaked hair was twisted up in a loose bun at the back of her head; mine hung dark and limp and unbrushed far past my shoulders. For the first time in a while, I found myself aware of and concerned about my own appearance.

"I've been the same," I answered. Why was everyone treating high school like it was years ago, instead of just weeks? "A little bored, I guess."

"Bored? God, I wish I could be bored! There's so much to do. This is our last summer before *college*, you know? Before life sets in!" She had no clue that I wasn't going to college, and that my life was never going to set in. How nice it must be, I mused, to have a life waiting for you, just beyond your grasp, until you graduated, when you were apparently allowed to reach out and grab it.

"Yeah..."

"So what brings you here?" she asked brightly, either

oblivious to my apathy or determined to be friendly. I would never understand those people, a separate species from my own.

"Uh, well, I'm going to be a volunteer for a camp called the Summer Siblings. There's supposed to be a meeting here."

Her eyes grew a little. "Yeah, this is where we're meeting! You're... I mean, have you...?"

"I'm new," I said. "This is my first summer."

"That's great," she said quickly. I eyed her suspiciously. Julie had something else to say, I could tell. I waited.

"It's just," she started. "Cara, I don't mean to hurt your feelings or be mean or anything, but you do realize that the summer after graduation is usually the last summer for siblings, not the first, right? I've been doing this since I was a freshman, but this is my last time. Mrs. Jameson told you about it, right? I mean, I guess you can always keep in touch with your sibling afterwards, but we can't exactly come back to the camp after this. It's... kind of weird to be starting now, don't you think?"

"Mrs. Jameson explained it all," I said quickly.

"I mean, I'm not criticizing you or anything," Julie continued. She ran a hand over the top of her head and adjusted her bun. "I'm sure Mrs. Jameson knows what she's doing; she's great. But if you don't mind me asking, what made you want to volunteer now?"

She looked down at me expectantly, but there was no way I was going to delve into the parameters of my therapy with Julie Singer. I shrugged at her with a little half-smile, hoping that would suffice as an answer.

"Well, I'm sure Mrs. Jameson knows what she's doing," Julie said again. "She's built this organization from the ground up. Hey, help me push some tables together?"

With that, she dropped the subject and flounced over to a corner of the coffee shop and started moving chairs away from a table.

"How many people are supposed to be here?" I asked as nonchalantly as I could while Julie counted chairs.

"Not sure," she said. "It's kind of just an open meeting for whoever wants to come. Super casual. Mrs. Jameson does this every year. We kind of brainstorm about meetings, and then she works out the dates and finalizes the details afterwards."

"If you had to guess," I prodded. "How many?"

Julie laughed. "I don't know. Ten, maybe?"

Ten. I could handle ten. But that didn't seem right. "I kind of thought the Summer Siblings would be bigger than that."

"Oh, my God, we're so much bigger than that!" Julie said, eyes wide. "Not everyone shows up to this meeting; that would be impossible. It's not mandatory, so only the really enthusiastic people usually come. I'd say there's probably about thirty or forty of us, from all over the school district. They're not all from Greenwood. And then there's that many little kids, and then there are a few counselors. And Mrs. Jameson."

"Counselors?"

"Yeah. There's a ratio of how many kids to adults you have to have. It's, like, a law or something. We're not exactly adults, so Mrs. Jameson has some camp counselors who kind of oversee stuff at our events. They're all really nice."

The bell over the cafe door jingled again. Julie looked up and waved over a petite girl with black hair cut into a sleek bob. The girl nodded in recognition, then went to the coffee counter and stared at the overhead menu.

"That's Isa Lin," Julie murmured to me. "She's really, really intense."

"Ah," I said, but was saved from further response by the café bell.

Julie frowned. "I think that's one of our guys. I can't ever remember, especially if they're not from our school."

The guy, lanky, dark, and sporting a crew cut, looked around the shop, then saw our table. Julie raised her hand in a hesitant half-wave. He approached us and grinned.

"Summer Siblings, right?" he asked.

"Right!" Julie said, instantly friendly. "You're... Darren, is that it?"

"Darien," he corrected her, though smiling. "It's okay, though. I forgot your name, too."

"Julie Singer," she said. "And this is Cara Carson."

"Hello, Julie Singer and Cara Carson," Darien grinned. He pulled out the chair opposite Julie and sat down. "How's it going?"

"Pretty good," Julie said, sliding on a smile and leaning forward on the table.

"Yeah," was the only contribution I could think to add.

"Can I get a hand over here?" the petite girl, Isa, called from the counter. Darien stood and went to her assistance. Other teenagers floated into the cafe, some heading straight for the table, others looking less certain. Finally, Mrs. Jameson herself appeared in the doorway, her jewelry jangling along with the bells.

"Cara, dear!" Mrs. Jameson said, slightly out of breath and smiling straight at me. I blushed at being singled out. "My word, but it's hot outside. I'm so glad you were able to make it!" Her fingers and painted nails fluttered in front of her face as she fanned herself. She was wearing another magnificent scarf, despite the heat, thin and gauzy though damp with sweat.

"Here I am," I said, staring down at my lap.

"Here you are," she echoed. Her eyes took in the others seated around the table. "Let's see, I'm sure you know Julie from Greenwood. And here we have Graham, and Nicole, and William—"

"Just Will," said the guy sitting across from me.

"Yes, dear, my apologies. Just Will, and who else, now? Emma, and Amber. Amber's a freshman, isn't that right, dear? So it's her first meeting, too."

Amber smiled at me. I tried to be a mirror, reflecting her face.

"And here's Isa and Darien now, if I'm not mistaken. I was wondering where Isa was!"

Isa and Darien walked over to our table, each carrying a small box of fresh pastries from the counter.

"Hello, Summer Siblings!" Isa proclaimed, setting her box down and passing out napkins. "Treats for everyone, to celebrate the start of another summer!" Julie glanced at me and gave me a slight eye roll but grabbed a donut anyway. Isa's hands were bony, flighty little birds, flitting between the boxes and napkins and other people, her fingers feathers that never settled.

"How generous of you, Isa, dear!" Mrs. Jameson beamed. "I was just introducing everyone at the table."

"I know everyone," Isa said breezily, then pointed at Amber and me. "Except you, and you. Are you freshmen?"

"I am," Amber said shyly.

"I'm not," I said, agitated. "I just graduated, actually."

Isa's eyes swiveled from me to Mrs. Jameson and back. "Then why are you joining the Summer Siblings now?"

My face reddened, but before I could say anything, the café bell tinkled again, and a well-built, tall boy walked in, pushing sunglasses on top of his head over thick, sable hair. The immature, teenage stubble from a few days of not shaving, pretending to be five o'clock shadow, darkened his chin. I recognized his face from school, and apparently, so did Julie and Mrs. Jameson, both of whom stared in surprise.

"Chase?" Mrs. Jameson called. The boy looked up and over at our table, his slack face unchanging. He hesitated, then approached us slowly. "How wonderful that you're joining us for our SS meeting today!"

"No, no," Chase said, holding his hands up and giving a half-grin. "I had no idea you guys were meeting today. Or meeting here. I just came by for some coffee. Total coincidence."

"Well, now that you're here, why don't you stay and chat with us?" Mrs. Jameson smiled. "We're just about to start discussing ideas for the summer."

"I really just came in for a coffee," Chase faltered. "I promise I'll be at the first official meeting."

"Please stay, dear," Mrs. Jameson said. "It would make an old lady like myself so happy. Everyone, this is Chase, another graduated senior who will be leaving us after this summer."

Chase pulled a face but didn't say anything. He dragged an empty chair over, but with no room left at the table, he pulled it around and sat behind me. I tensed up.

"I'll just observe," he commented.

Mrs. Jameson smiled at him. "We're glad you're here,

Chase. What a lovely surprise! Now, what was I saying?"

"I was wondering why Cara is just joining now," Isa said clearly.

"No need to worry about that, Isa," Mrs. Jameson said gently. "Cara and I have already talked."

Isa caught my eye. I flushed but refused to look away.

"It's kind of a long story," I said. "But if you're looking for a reason, um, I'm not going to college, and I wanted something to do with my time, and we kind of agreed this would be a good thing to do, even if it only lasts a summer."

My explanation hung ungracefully over our table, a marionette with an unskilled puppeteer who tangled up all the strings. Isa continued to stare, a single eyebrow raised in doubt.

"You're not going to college?" Chase inquired from just over my right shoulder.

"Leave her alone, Chase," Julie instructed. "We're here to talk about Summer Siblings."

"No, it's okay," I said, determined not to back down, embarrassed though I was. "I didn't apply anywhere. It just didn't seem like the place for me to be." I didn't mention how much I was regretting my decision. Without looking at Mrs. Jameson, I kept talking, twisting the truth just a little. "So I decided to do some volunteer work while I planned my next move, and I did some research on volunteer opportunities around town. I really liked the idea of being a big sister, but I... don't feel quite qualified for the national level. So I talked to Mrs. Jameson about maybe helping out with the Summer Siblings."

"And we thank you for your enthusiasm, Cara, dear," Mrs. Jameson said, with a note of finality.

Like a switch had been flipped, Isa's defensive energy dropped, and she smiled sweetly at me. "Well, welcome to the Summer Siblings, Cara. I'm sure you'll love being a sibling. We have so much fun."

"Thanks," stumbled out of my mouth.

"Moving on," Mrs. Jameson said, smoothly authoritative. "We're here to pick dates for the summer events. So, my dears, who has any ideas?"

"I think a good mixture of activities would be best," Isa said immediately. "Structured stuff on some days and more free time on others."

Darien nodded. "I like that."

"Excellent," said Mrs. Jameson. She flipped through a large day planner. "What sort of activities, specifically?"

"The park is free. We could take the kids there and just let them run around for a while," Nicole suggested.

"We do the park every summer," Isa said, but Mrs. Jameson held up her hand.

"The park is a favorite because it works," she said. "Thank you, Nicole, dear. Other ideas?"

"I thought maybe we could go to the planetarium," Isa said quickly. "I already called, and they said they would be willing to give us a group discount if you talk with them."

"I can take care of that easily," Mrs. Jameson said while scribbling in her planner. "Let's keep going with the planetarium. Is that something you dears think the children will enjoy?"

"I'm not going to college, either," Chase whispered, very quietly, near my ear. The back of my neck tingled with his proximity. I took a moment to marvel at how sad it was that I considered someone whispering in my ear about his choice to forgo higher education to be semi-intimate.

"Why?" I asked quietly.

"Because," he said back. I kept my eyes on Mrs. Jameson but turned slightly towards him, anticipating the rest of his reason, but that seemed to be it.

I wished I weren't in the middle of the table, surrounded by enthusiasm. I wished I could trade chairs with Chase, looking in from behind. With nothing to contribute, I began an extreme contemplation of my hands.

The conversation continued, ebbing and flowing. My ears began to fill with the familiar buzz, building a wall between myself and the rest of the world. I watched everyone's interaction like it was a nature show, something vaguely familiar, but overall animalistic and foreign to me. Ms. Wells would want me to stop this mindset and make myself present, but I stayed on the edge, fascinated and removed.

"Alright," Mrs. Jameson finally said. At her voice, I shook my head to clear the fuzziness and tried to pay attention. "A trip to the park, the planetarium, the movies, the aquarium, an arts and crafts day, the zoo, the science museum, and a camp-wide kickball day. I think these are all wonderful ideas. I'll work out specific dates with the counselors, who will be in touch with you soon. Let's talk about what you're looking forward to, or for those who have done this before, what you think we could improve. Cara, would you share what you told me during our meeting about what being a sibling means to you?"

All eyes flicked towards me. My heart sped up. My mental wall crumbled, panic rising in its place. I couldn't repeat that speech in front of everyone.

"I have to go," I said, over-loudly. I stood up, my chair screeching against the floor. I'd walk home if I had to.

"Do you really, Cara, dear?" Mrs. Jameson asked, looking a little startled.

"We're not done with the meeting," Isa blurted.

"Yes. I have to go," I repeated stupidly, but I didn't move.

"Alright," said Julie, kindly interceding. If she were fazed by my sudden aptitude for drama, she didn't show it. I was beginning to feel grateful for it, beginning to remember why we had been friends so long ago. "Thanks for coming to our meeting, Cara."

"Thanks," I mumbled. The others nodded in somewhat earnest agreement. I stumbled a little trying to extricate myself from the tangle of the chairs. Chase reached up a hand to catch me, but I balanced myself on the back of his chair and moved towards the door.

"Just one minute, dear," Mrs. Jameson said, rummaging through her bag again. I felt exceptionally exposed. She handed me a sealed manila envelope across the table.

"That's all the information about your new sibling," she said. "So you can get in touch before the first event, you see."

"Thanks," I said to her. Then I raised my head slightly and addressed the group. "Thanks, guys."

"Goodbye, dear," Mrs. Jameson said. Tripping over my own feet, I clutched the envelope and stumbled out of the coffee shop and away from the Summer Siblings.

CHAPTER 5

"Cara, *please*. Please, take a breath, so we can talk."

"I c-can't," I managed to choke out. Tears were spilling down my face. Actual tears. I swiped at them angrily, embarrassed by their rivers.

Audie Wells pulled a tissue out of its box and handed it to me. "This is good, Cara. You may not believe it, but this emotion is good. You're looking at something in the face instead of hiding from it. You're confronting it. But the only way we can work through this is if you take some deep breaths and try to calm down. Let's talk about it. Take a deep breath, Cara."

I drew a shuddering breath and clenched my jaw, holding the tissue to my face. "Okay. Okay. I'm okay."

"That's right. You're okay," Ms. Wells assured me. "Can you tell me what made you ask for an emergency meeting?"

"I'm so sorry," I sniffed. "I shouldn't have called you on your cell."

"That's exactly why I gave you my cell number. For

emergencies. So let's make good use of this time that you asked for and figure out what the problem is. "

"Right." I thrust Mrs. Jameson's manila envelope at Ms. Wells. "I can't do this."

She took the envelope hesitatingly. "Do I have your permission to open this, Cara?"

I stood up angrily and grabbed it back from her. "Just look at it!" I unfastened the clip and dumped the contents onto the small table between us. Sheets of paper slipped out and slid across the tabletop. Somewhat frantically, I leafed through them until I pulled out a glossy photograph. A young girl beamed up at the camera, her eyes bright against her sepia-tinted skin.

Ms. Wells looked at the picture, then at me. "Who is this, Cara?"

I stared blankly at the photo. "That's my Summer Sibling."

Ms. Wells picked up one of the papers and glanced at it. "Gabrielle Moore. She looks adorable, Cara."

"She's a girl," I told Ms. Wells. "A girl. A sister."

Ms. Wells slowly uncapped her pen and pressed it against her notebook. "Do you want to tell me why this is a problem, Cara?"

I didn't answer.

"May I take a guess?"

I nodded.

"Did you think that you would be assigned a little brother?"

I hated myself. I nodded.

"Let's talk about this."

"What..." my voice faltered. I tried again. "What is there

to talk about? I'm so stupid. I signed up for the Summer Siblings with an ulterior motive, even though I told Mrs. Jameson that wasn't true. I wanted a little brother. I got a little sister. I'm awful. I freaked out at first because I thought you wanted me to replace Aaron, and now I'm freaking out because I think maybe I wanted that, too."

"Take a breath, Cara," Ms. Wells said. She extended a reassuring hand out towards me. "What else?"

"And I thought it would be just me and a kid, not an entire group of people I have to be around. I can't do it. I'm in way over my head. I didn't think this through. You want to know how the first meeting ended for me? I walked out just because Mrs. Jameson asked me a question. I can't do the group activities, I can't do the talking to other people, I can't do the role model act, I can't do the sister thing, *I can't do it.*" My pitch bubbled over into hysteria, a tea kettle's steaming shriek.

"Breathe, Cara." Ms. Wells' voice was calm and steady. "Okay? This is good. Keep going."

"I don't want to do it," I told her.

"You changed your verb."

"What?"

"You changed from saying you can't to saying you don't want to."

I frowned. "I don't want to because I can't."

"I really don't believe that, Cara," Ms. Wells said firmly. "I think there's a beautiful little girl out there who could really use a big sister, and I think you're the perfect one for the job."

I didn't say anything.

"Cara?" Ms. Wells peered at me until I met her eye. "I need you to understand that this opportunity is not a chance to try and replace Aaron. You were upset by that at first, but now it seems like it might have gotten a little twisted around."

"I know," I muttered, dropping my gaze.

"You don't *have* to do it," she continued. "I can't force you to do anything you don't want to do. But I would like you to seriously consider each side. If you don't do it, and if you do. You have so much love in your heart left from Aaron. And I'm not saying that you can't stop giving that love to Aaron. But you can give it elsewhere, too."

I looked at Ms. Wells in silence.

"It will be difficult," Ms. Wells said patiently. "But I think you'll find it will be worth it, in the long run."

I kept my eyes on her.

"Will you do it, Cara?"

Slow, long, calming breaths. I imagined my lungs as the moon, steadily pulling the tides of my breath in and out. "Okay."

"Not to find a substitute for Aaron. To help yourself and to help Gabrielle."

"Right."

"I'm so proud of you, Cara. I think you can really make an impact."

I cleared my throat and tried to pretend I didn't just have a mortifying breakdown over a little girl I had never met. "I still don't know what I'm doing. The first event is coming up soon, I think. I don't know what to do."

"I have a suggestion, Cara, if you'd like to hear it."

I shrugged.

"This would be a good chance for you to get to know Gabrielle before you go out with the group. Why don't you call her right now? Ask her to do something prior to the first

SS event." Ms. Wells handed me one of the papers from my envelope. I squinted at the text on it, finally discerning someone's address and phone number. Contact information.

"I can't."

"You can," Ms. Wells said. "Why don't you use the phone on my desk? I think I need to check on something in the waiting room. You know, make sure the magazines are up to date." She gave me a warm smile. "I'll be right outside the door if you need me."

"What do I say? Tell me what to say," I pleaded, fully aware of how desperate I sounded.

"Cara, I'm not here to give you all the answers to life," Ms. Wells said firmly, though kindly. "I'm confident you'll handle this perfectly." With that, she stood and left, leaving me alone with the phone.

The room wanted to swallow me. I walked slowly to the desk and lowered myself into the cushioned office chair. On the other side of the wall, I could hear Ms. Wells moving around the waiting room purposefully. Her desk was very tidy, with a specific place for everything. I pulled a pad of sticky notes towards me and took a pen from a beautifully painted ceramic mug. If I didn't write down everything I wanted to say, I wouldn't be able to say anything at all.

There are people who cannonball into cold pools, rip off bandages, say hard goodbyes quickly and easily and are done with it. I was never one of those people. It took twelve sticky notes to write out my little script (with all possible answers to all possible questions). I couldn't hear Ms. Wells anymore; she was obviously waiting for me to finish with a call I hadn't even started. The phone sat, silent and still, resting in its cradle. I hadn't used a landline like this in a long time.

I finally lifted the phone and held it to my ear. A dull dial tone. Deliberately and laboriously, I pressed the numbers, reading them off the contact sheet. A shrill ring rattled my skull. Another. Another. Too many. Maybe I'd be saved by the blessing of voicemail.

"Hello?"

Damn.

"Hi, this is Cara Carson," I recited, my heart pounding. "I'm Gabrielle's new big sister from the Summer Siblings camp."

"The what?"

"The— the Summer Siblings," I faltered, flipping through my notes. "Mrs. Earla Jameson should have— she was supposed to call you."

"Oh." The voice sounded flat, almost uninterested.

"Are... are you Gabrielle's mother?" I asked hesitatingly. I hoped she couldn't hear the shaking of nerves in my own voice. "Mrs. Moore?"

"Yeah. Earla said someone was going to do stuff with Gabby for the summer. Is that what this is about?"

"That's right," I said, relieved, and back on track with my notes. "So, um, I was wondering if we could find a date where I could come get Gabrielle and take her out for ice cream. It doesn't have to be ice cream, we could go anywhere—"

"Ice cream's fine. Anytime is fine," said Mrs. Moore. "You have our address?"

"Yes," I said. "Mrs. Jameson gave it to me."

"Alright, come get her whenever you want." With that, the line went dead, leaving me alone again with the dial tone. I still had questions, but I had completed the task at hand. Surprised, but not displeased, I let the peaceful silence of the office settle around me, letting myself rest in the knowledge that I had accomplished something even as small as a phone call. After a moment, I pushed myself away from the desk, collected my belongings, and headed for the waiting room.

Ms. Wells was peering intently at a crossword puzzle in the back of a magazine. She looked up as I entered the room.

"How'd it go?" she asked.

"I guess it went okay," I answered. "I talked to Gabrielle's mom. She said I could come get her whenever I wanted, but she hung up before I could pick a date."

Ms. Wells nodded her head and folded her hands. "I see."

"So, I guess I'll be seeing Gabrielle soon."

"I think this will be a wonderful and hopefully healing experience."

"Mm," I said, noncommittal. "Well. Thanks again for meeting with me like this, Ms. Wells. I'm sorry I... overreacted."

"Not a problem, Cara," she said genuinely. "Please give me a call if you need anything else. Journal about this. Try to frame it positively. Remind yourself how good this can be."

This is going to be a disaster. At least my meltdown with Ms. Wells today proves that Aaron and I were born into the right roles. In no universe should I ever be a big sister.

Aaron always waited two days after calling a girl he liked before following up with another call or date. I ungraciously allowed three days to pass after my phone call, stewing away moodily in my room. On the fourth day, guilt began to gnaw at my insides, reminding me that a little girl was expecting me to come take her on an adventure, however small. By lunchtime, I had made the monumental move of getting dressed, and a full hour later, I pulled on my sneakers and managed to get myself into my car.

My thoughts swarmed around me and took the passenger seat, backseat drivers that would not let me think straight. *Be present.* I tried to concentrate only on the road. The drive to Gabrielle Moore's house took me across town to a neighborhood with small but sturdy brick houses, many of which had colorful gardens out front. I slowed down in the residential streets, peering out my window at the lines of numbers identifying the homes. When I finally reached her house, I pulled into the driveway and sat there for a bit, the AC in my car still running.

What would I even say to her? What could I possibly do to make her trust me, like me, want to spend time with me?

I removed the key from the ignition, unbuckled my seatbelt, and opened the car door—slow, deliberate actions. A few minutes crawled by before the heat really got to me. As I slammed the car door shut, the door to the house burst open almost simultaneously. A little girl stared at me expectantly from the stoop.

"Are you Cara?" she demanded. She barreled down the front sidewalk and stood in front of me, her head level with my hip, leaning back to see my face.

"Yep. I'm Cara," I said uneasily, feeling accosted. "Are you—"

"I'm Gabby," she interrupted. "Momma said you were gonna come get me! And you're here! You came! I like your shirt."

"Thank you," I said. Gabrielle was wearing a shockingly bright pink dress, a little jumper with two big white buttons on the shoulder straps. "I like your dress."

Without acknowledging she'd heard me, she spun around and raced back to her house.

"Cara's here!" she squealed into the open doorway. "I'm going with Cara, Momma!"

She paused, as if listening for a response, but I didn't hear anything. After a moment, she closed the door carefully, then ran back towards my car, her white sandals slapping against the sidewalk with each step. Her hair was a small puffball cloud around her head, and her hazel eyes glowed expectantly. She had an unexpected spray of freckles on her dusky cheeks. I couldn't help it— I smiled down at her. Gabrielle was adorable.

"I'm ready!" she announced. I looked towards her house and wondered if I should go in and meet her mother. Ms. Wells would want me to. My own mother would want me to. Every manner I had ever learned growing up insisted that I do. Shamefacedly, I turned from the Moore house to my car.

"Would you like to get some ice cream with me?" I asked Gabrielle. I wondered how strong her sense of stranger danger was. In my ears, I sounded forward and even a little creepy, but her face split into a nearly manic grin, showing all her tiny teeth.

"Ice cream!" she shrieked, then dashed around me to the front passenger seat.

"Um, backseat for you, Gabby," I said, her shortened name awkward on my tongue, the authoritative order uncomfortable in my mouth. Should I have a car seat for her?

How old did kids have to be to not need a car seat? What if she didn't listen to me?

But she did, moving down the side of the car, pulling open the back door, and clambering in. I got in behind the wheel.

"How come I have to sit back here? I can't see you," she said, not complaining, but genuinely interested.

"I don't want the car's airbags to crush you in case there's an accident," my mouth babbled without my permission. *Oh, my God. Why would you tell that to a child, Cara?* But she didn't seem affected. "And I can see you, in my rearview mirror." I adjusted the mirror, angling it slightly downwards, and raised my eyebrows at her reflection. She laughed and made the same face back at me. "Um, put your seatbelt on, please, before we go."

She buckled herself in without question. I clicked my own buckle into its slot and backed out onto the road.

"Where're we going?" asked Gabby.

"For ice cream, remember?"

"Yeah, but *where?*"

"Do you have somewhere specific in mind?"

"Let's go to Pop's Ice Cream Parlor," she said, kicking her feet gently against the center console, looking out the window. "Momma took me there once."

"Okay. I know where that is." I made a quick U-turn on the main road and drove in the opposite direction. Silence ballooned within the small interior of the car.

"So… what grade will you be in when school starts up?" I asked, even though I already knew the answer from her information sheet.

She held up two fingers for me to see in the rearview

mirror. "Second grade! And I'm seven and one quarter years old."

"Wow," I said. "Are you excited about this summer?"

"Yes." Apparently bored by our lackluster conversation, she started humming a tune. I tapped my fingers against the steering wheel and tried to remember what it had been like to be seven. What it had been like to be a little sister. What it had been like to move through childhood with Aaron. We were riding bikes together, we were flying on our swing set in the backyard, he was climbing a tree and I was throwing pine cones at him...

"Turn left here," Gabby instructed. I glanced in the mirror at her and flipped on my turn signal.

"Yeah, I know," I said gently. "You're pretty good with directions."

"This is my *fay-vo-rite* place," she emphasized.

"I thought you'd only been here once."

"I see it every time we come home from school," she clarified. "My school bus drives right past here."

We turned into the parking lot of a slightly run-down, small shopping plaza. The little ice cream shop was wedged between a dry cleaner and a nail salon. I brought the car to a stop and announced cheerily, "We're here!" Gabby squealed from the backseat, fumbled with her seatbelt, and flung herself out of the car. I found myself smiling as she ran to the store's glass door, then back to me, then back to the door.

"Ice cream!" she cried, jumping and clapping her hands together. I reached over her head and opened the door for her; she ran inside while I stood on the threshold, letting the blast of cool air ground me. I joined her at the counter, where she was standing on tiptoes to peer through the glass into the tubs of ice cream just out of reach.

"Do you want me to read you the names of the flavors?"

"I know what I want," she said. "I just have to find it."

"What kind do you want?"

"Bananzas."

I puzzled over that for a minute. "Do you mean 'bananas' or 'bonanza?'"

"It didn't have bananas in it."

"What was in it?"

"It was vanilla ice cream and it had M&Ms in it and chocolate too. And Momma let me get sprinkles on it."

I motioned for an employee behind the counter to come over. She looked younger than me, with a smooth face and curly dark hair. I wondered if lots of ice cream was good for your skin. Or maybe she totally avoided eating the ice cream, and that was why her skin was so nice. Maybe if you worked with something long enough, you got sick of it, and never wanted it. I had never worked any sort of job that would allow me to find out. "Do you have a flavor called Bonanza?"

"Hm." She ran her eyes over the many tubs. "That doesn't sound familiar to me. Let me go check our full list in the back." I waited while Gabby continued to peek into every tub, looking for her flavor.

"I'm sorry," said the girl, stepping back behind the counter. She scrunched up her face in an apologetic kind of way. "I think the flavor you're looking for was called Candy Crunch Bonanza. That used to be one of our flavors, but our owner comes up with new ones so often that we trade them out all the time. We haven't had it for almost a year."

I was a little confused by that. "Gabby, when was the last time you came here?"

"Last summer."

I couldn't believe she remembered not only the place and time, but also the flavor and name (almost) of ice cream she had eaten. I crouched down so I was at her eye level. "Gabby, they don't have that flavor here anymore. Do you want to pick a new flavor?"

She looked at me with sad eyes, her bottom lip curling out like a flower petal. "Why don't they have it?"

"They change the flavors all the time," I said. "Here's what I think we should do. You tell me what flavor I should get, and then you pick a flavor for yourself. If you don't like yours, you can have mine."

"*Two* flavors?"

"Yep."

"Oh my gosh!" Clearly, Gabby's main method of communication was through squeals, but surprisingly, it didn't bother me. I stood back and let Gabby take control as she pointed out two flavors to the employee.

"One Cotton Candy Carnival and one Double Chocolate Brownie Delight," smiled the girl. "How many scoops do you want, sweetie?"

"One scoop?" she said, turning to me with wide sand dollar eyes.

"Double scoops, please," I said to the employee, winking at Gabby. She let out another shriek and spread her arms out wide, as if nothing in the world could be better than four scoops of two flavors of ice cream. The girl behind the counter nudged the ice cream into warm waffle cones, wafting the smell throughout the store. I paid with cash and dumped the change into the tip jar.

"Let's eat outside, Gabby," I said, handing her the cone

full of blindingly pink ice cream, even brighter than her dress. There were small pieces of purple candy worked in among the pinkness of it all. I hoped that she meant for me to have the other one, which seemed pretty normal, just chocolate with bits of brownie and nuts. I grabbed some napkins and pushed open the door with my shoulder, directing Gabby towards a small, rusted iron table with a faded umbrella near the sidewalk.

Gabby got right to work on her cone, biting straight into the ice cream rather than licking it. Her feet, high off the ground, swung merrily in short arcs as she attacked her treat with as much ferocity as a seven year old could manage. I ate mine slowly, ignoring the drips that ran their way down the cone in the heavy heat.

"Did you want to try any of mine?" I asked.

"No, mine is *great*," she responded enthusiastically. "Deeee-licious!" She had already started munching on the soggy edges of the cone, pink smeared around her mouth like lipstick.

"I'm sorry you couldn't get that flavor you liked," I commented. She didn't answer but continued to gnaw at her cone. I wondered whether or not she was subject to brain freeze.

After a moment, I asked, in the gentlest tone I could muster, "So, you haven't been here in over a year, huh?"

"Yeah." I couldn't tell if her sudden drop in chattiness was due to a sore subject or because her extreme dedication to the sugar.

"It must have been some really good ice cream, if you could remember its name a whole year later."

"I remembered 'cause it was a treat for a bad day."

"Oh yeah?" I was afraid to probe further, almost afraid that she would innocently divulge the reason she was in the Summer Siblings camp without realizing it, leaving me to bear the burden. I wasn't sure how much I wanted to know.

"Yeah. Momma brought me and Logan here to make us feel better."

"Ice cream makes me feel better, too." I hesitated. What could be the worst response? Her parents lost their jobs? The family was on welfare? I decided to go for it. "What happened?"

"The baby died."

I froze. An enormous drop of melted ice cream fell into my lap. I barely felt it. "What?"

"Momma was gonna have a baby, but the baby died right after it was borned, and so Momma took us here for ice cream and to tell us." Gabby continued to chomp away at her cone. "I got the Bananzas with pink sprinkles."

"Gabrielle," I breathed. I didn't say I was sorry, because I knew enough of death and dying to know that that disyllabic word was the most useless thing in the universe. I tried to mold my own experience with loss down to a second grader's level. "I'm… sure you were very sad."

She looked up from her ice cream. "Yeah, I guess so. I was sad because Momma was sad. She cried and cried and didn't even eat her ice cream. She let me and Logan eat it. I was sad we didn't get to meet the baby, but also because Momma was crying."

I sat in silence, watching the little girl as she chased her dripping, melting ice cream down the cone, licking each of her fingers. "My brother, Aaron, left when I was 14."

She looked up at me. "Oh."

I had lost my appetite. The remaining chocolate ice cream ran down the mushy cone and pooled in the palm of my hand, like a mud puddle.

"Do you miss him?" she asked nonchalantly, as if this were a normal conversation.

"So—" my voice caught. "So much. It hurts everyday."

"My daddy left too," she said. "A little while after the baby."

It occurred to me that my verb usage was a little vague to a seven year old. "Gabby, when I say my brother left, I meant to say..." I cleared my throat and whispered, "He died. Like the baby."

"Oh. Was he a baby, too?"

I shook my head. I felt an immense connection with the little girl at this moment. In the back of my mind, I imagined Mrs. Jameson and Ms. Wells hand picking Gabrielle Moore for me, nodding as they put together pieces of a puzzle.

"Did you cry when he died?" Gabby asked.

"Yeah," I said softly. "I cried a lot."

"I cried a lot when my daddy left."

"I can imagine," I said. I looked past Gabby, at the mostly empty parking lot behind her. "It's funny how we cry even though we know that won't bring them back. I guess there's just nothing else for us to do."

"The sadness has to get out somehow," said Gabby. "So it comes out in tears. And sometimes that's just how you have to let it out. How else could you get rid of it and stop being sad?"

I just looked at her. "Sometimes, it takes a while before you can stop being sad."

"Maybe," she said, dismissing the subject and reaching for a flimsy napkin. Her cone was gone, and all that remained of the ice cream was on her face. I looked down at my sticky hands, then up at her. My heart swelled.

"Hey," I said, clearing my throat. "How about we go get our nails painted next door?"

"*Really?*"

"Yep. Let's go get manicures."

"Yay, yay, yay!" She cheered along with each step as she bounced (and I walked) to the store on the other side of the ice cream shop. Walk-ins welcome. A woman inside brought us to an entire wall filled with bottles of nail polish, a world of colors captured in glass and sealed shut.

As I expected, Gabby flounced right up to the shelf and chose neon pink, the brightest available bottle, without a moment's hesitation. She shook it expectantly, then turned to me. "What color are you gonna get?"

I considered the shelves before me. It had been a long time since I'd gotten my nails done or even painted them myself at home. I reached for a deep navy. "I like this dark blue."

She shook her head and moved my hand to the same row her pink polish had come from. "Get this blue. It's like the sky without clouds. Plus, it has glitter in it."

"Okay." I smiled at her and accepted the bright little bottle she had pointed out, an enormous round sapphire with a black cap. I figured I could take it off with polish remover when I got home.

I didn't take it off until it chipped beyond recognition two weeks later.

CHAPTER 6

I only spent a couple of hours with Gabby, but it feels like I've known her so much longer. What I don't know is how I'm supposed to help her, or what Ms. Wells expects me to do. What kind of a big sister am I supposed to be? How am I supposed to make Gabby's life better? What exactly am I supposed to do?

Five days later, my cell phone rang with a number I didn't recognize. I answered it anyway, an unusual action for me.

"Hello?"

"May I speak with Cara?"

"This is she," I said politely. I didn't recognize the male voice.

"Hi, Cara. My name's Sebastian. I'm your assigned Summer Siblings counselor."

"My assigned counselor?"

The man laughed. "It's nothing serious. We all have calling lists that Earla delegates so that everyone can be up to date about events. You just happen to be in my group, so you're on my calling list."

"Earla?"

"Earla Jameson."

"Right," I said, trying not to sound stupid or too many steps behind. "I knew that."

"Yep. Earla originally had you on Audie's calling list, but Audie thought maybe... well, I'm getting off topic. Anyway, you're on my list now."

"Audie? Like, Audie Wells?" My heart pounded conspiratorially. "She works for the Summer Siblings?"

"No one really works for it. We volunteer," Sebastian said. "But I probably shouldn't have opened my big mouth about that. I'm sure you'll see her at the events. You can talk to her in person then."

"Yeah, I'm sure I'll see her," I mumbled. Not necessarily at a Summer Siblings event, but I'd see her.

"Well, I've got the dates for you, if you want to write them down. If you want to use Earla as a job reference or something, you have to attend at least half of the events. You ready for the dates?"

I glanced at the calendar that had been hanging on my wall, frozen in October for the last three years. Thirty-one blank faces stared back at me. I gently pulled the bottom corner up and peeked at November.

"Cara? You still there?"

Crap. Be present. "Yeah, sorry." I pulled the calendar off the wall and curled it into my wastebasket. Then I pulled a fresh piece of paper to me. "I'm ready."

A short while later, I dialed Gabrielle's house number. I wasn't quite as nervous for this phone call, but I still felt a little uneasy. Her mother answered.

"Mrs. Moore? This is Cara Carson, from—"

"Summer Siblings. Yeah. She's been talking non-stop about you."

"Oh?" I didn't know how to respond to that. "That's, uh, nice to hear. She's a great girl."

"She is."

"Well, I, uh, I have a list of dates for the Summer Siblings stuff. I wanted to tell them to you now, so you can let me know if she'll be able to make any of them."

"She'll be there."

"But—" I stopped short. "Don't you want to hear the dates?"

"Just come get Gabby whenever," she said, and abruptly hung up. Half a minute later, I realized I was still holding the phone to my ear, unsettled by the sudden end to the conversation. I thoughtfully gazed at the list of scribbled dates, then tacked it onto the wall where my calendar had hung, purposeless, for so long. Suddenly, the blank fortune pinned to my bulletin board next to the dates didn't seem nearly as enticing as before.

Gabby's decibel-shattering squeals of joy greeted me upon my arrival at her house for the first Summer Siblings event: a trip to the park. It confused me that I, of all people, could inspire such a reaction, but I felt a genuine smile on my face as she catapulted into my car. Again, I wondered if I should go in and see her mother, but again, I chickened out.

"We're going to the park! We're going to the park!" Gabby chanted. She was wearing a bright red shirt and shockingly yellow shorts, both of which clashed enormously with the pink headband jammed into her hair.

I had been to this park, nearly half an hour from Gabby's house, countless times as a child, but never without Aaron. Memories played like a filmstrip across my mind, rolling in front of my eyes. Feeding the ducks, Aaron munching on the stale bread. Hiding under a wooden bridge, hands pressed over our mouths, trying not to laugh and give away our hiding place. Lying in the tall grass, swatting away mosquitoes, scratching at bug bites. I was startled to find myself pulling into a parking spot, apparently having autopiloted the whole drive there.

Not okay, Cara. Not safe, I reprimanded myself. *Be present.* I looked out through the windshield at families doing family things in the green space before us. Gabby had already wriggled out of her seatbelt and was waiting for me outside the car.

"Caraaa!" she sang. "Come *on*, Care-uh! We're *here!*"

My fingers tightened around the steering wheel. Through glazed eyes, I could just make out Julie and Isa at the gazebo in the distance.

"I said, we're here!" Gabby yelled from outside. She opened my car door, reached across my lap, and clicked my seatbelt buckle. The strap slithered across my body and caught on my left arm. Gabby laughed, like this was a game, like this was normal. When I still didn't move, she leaned over and started peeling each of my fingers off of the steering wheel. She counted each one as I loosened my grip.

"Ten!" she chirped. "Now you're free. Let's go."

My hands drooped, purposeless, in my lap. I inhaled deeply and pulled my keys from the ignition. Aaron's lucky

ERICA KELLY TRAN

penny keychain jingled against the metal. I held the penny as
tightly as I had the steering wheel, pressing the pad of my
thumb against the star cutout. Gabby grabbed my free hand
and pulled me across the asphalt to the grass.

"Okay," I said, more to myself than to Gabby. "Okay.
Head that way, Gabby. Towards the gazebo. See everyone?"

"Is it a party?"

"Something like that." Approaching the gazebo revealed
how many Summer Siblings were actually there, which made
my heart speed up with nerves. The small meeting at the
coffee shop had made me uneasy; this was enough to make
me downright sick. A few faces from Greenwood stood out to
me, but I wasn't sure if that was harmful or helpful. Most of
the teenagers were unfamiliar, members from the other
schools in the district. The only thing everyone in the area
had in common seemed to be a kid attached to their side.

"Hey, Cara!" Julie called from under the shade of the
gazebo. A little girl in a polka dot dress peeked out from
behind her.

"*Kimmy!*" cried Gabby in recognition, running towards
her. Kimmy shrieked in delight. They clasped hands, fingers
woven together like a multi-colored basket, chattering at an
indecipherable high speed.

"Looks like they know each other," Julie smiled.

"Looks like it," I echoed. I turned slightly and looked out
at all of the Siblings playing together. Scattered throughout
the teenagers were adults, all of whom were sporting lime
green shirts with *Summer Siblings* emblazoned on their chests.

"Are those the counselors?" I asked. Julie nodded. "Do
you know which one is Sebastian?"

"He's over there," Julie said, waving at a lime-shirt-clad

man with a patchy goatee. He waved back, then turned his attention to what appeared to be an intense game of tag. I looked around for Ms. Wells, but I couldn't pick her out amidst the chaotic activity. Frisbees flew by, kites hovered above heads, kids lounged on picnic blankets eating snacks...

"I didn't bring anything for Gabby to do," I said in an undertone to Julie. It hadn't occurred to me to provide any sort of extra entertainment.

"That's okay," Julie said reassuringly. "There's a swingset nearby, or you can just enjoy the sunshine."

As if she could hear my insufficiency, Isa breezed over to us. "Hello, girls. How's everyone doing?"

"We're good," Julie said.

"Do you guys need anything? I brought a whole bag of extra toys and things if people need them," Isa said, casting a quick glance at me.

"Actually, yeah," I said, pushing down the irritation that welled up in me. I could overcome it for Gabby. "That'd be great."

"Let me go get it!" Isa said, smiling.

Julie waited for Isa to leave. "You know, she's not really the leader or anything. It's not like we have a club president, even if she acts like it. She just does this extra stuff to feel important. You don't have to cater to her."

"I know," I said quickly. "But I just... I kind of want to, I don't know, provide for Gabby. I want to be there for her. You know?"

"Yeah, I get that," Julie conceded. Isa returned, laden with several canvas tote bags in the crooks of her arms and a large cardboard box. A girl carrying another box trailed behind her. She looked to be slightly older than Gabby, but her shoes had Velcro straps on them, the kind you found on younger kids.

"Cara, this is my Summer Sibling, Nina. She's going to be in fourth grade, and she's very smart! Julie, you remember Nina, of course," Isa said.

"Hi, Nina. Your shoes are so cool!" said Julie sweetly.

"They really are," I agreed. "So, fourth grade. I guess I didn't think about how the kids aren't all the same age."

"Nope," said Isa. She placed a hand lovingly on Nina's shoulder, who beamed up at Isa. "But Nina's the smartest fourth grader I know!"

I was tempted to ask Isa just how many fourth graders she knew.

"And you're a senior now. In high school. That's so *cool*," Nina said, her voice full of admiration.

"The coolest thing," Isa said, crouching down to hug Nina, "is that we're both sisters."

Was this how people talked in real life? Had I been so far removed from casual conversation in the past three years that I had forgotten how to interpret interactions? I marveled at Isa's bird hands, which were smoothing back Nina's dark hair. I glanced at Julie, to see if I could garner a hint on how to respond, but she had turned from Isa and was calling to Kimmy.

"Feel free to take whatever you want," Isa said, indicating the box and bags at her feet.

"Thanks," I said. I crouched down, digging through the bags, sorting through old jump ropes, partially deflated bouncy balls, and various other toys I recognized from my own childhood.

"This is a lot of stuff," I commented.

"Yeah, I just went through our garage," she replied. "My dad never gets rid of anything."

I couldn't think of anything else to say, so I pretended to be absorbed in examining a decrepit box of chipped sidewalk chalk. Flipping open the lid, I checked for a pink stick— it was worn down and dull at the edges, but it would work.

"Mind if I take the chalk, Isa?" I asked.

"Go for it!" she said enthusiastically, smiling. I thanked her and turned to where I had left Gabby. She was lying flat on her stomach, picking at pieces of grass that had pushed through cracks in the cement.

"Look, Gabby," I said, showing her the chalk. "Want to draw with me?"

"Is there pink chalk? I want the pink chalk," she demanded, scrambling up. "Can we draw here?"

"Let's go over there," I said, gently leading her away from the gazebo and over to a sidewalk that cut through the grass, offset from the center of activity. It was just far enough to be somewhat removed, but still close enough to be in the vicinity of the group.

"I'm going to draw a pony," Gabby informed me. "Maybe a horse, too. Ponies and horses are different."

"What should I draw?"

"Um…" Gabby thought, then pulled out a blue chalk stick and handed it to me. "Draw some flowers for the pony to eat."

"Do ponies eat flowers?"

"Yes," she said definitively.

"Okay," I said, touching the blue chalk to the sidewalk, fragments of color crumbling away. I swept it across the cement in clumsy circles, sketching out a fat flower. Gabby nodded in approval.

"Keep going," she instructed, then began to draw what I had to believe was a horse, all wobbly ovals and thin lines. I smiled at her concentration and continued to draw my blue flowers, a funny daisy chain in chalk. With my back to the gazebo, I could hear shrieks of joy and gleeful shouts, but I couldn't differentiate between the teenagers and the kids.

"Heads up!"

A green and yellow knit ball, about the size of my fist, landed on the edge of one of my flowers. I reached out and grabbed it, seeing where it had smudged the chalk, as if it had knocked off a petal, then looked around for its owner.

"Well, if it isn't Cara Carson and her little sis!"

I held back a groan as I saw Adam Beck and a young boy trotting across the grass to our sidewalk.

"Hey," I said flatly.

"Sorry about that," Adam said, reaching us and holding out a hand for the ball. I twirled it once in my fingers before giving it to him; it felt like a soft, tiny bean bag.

"What kind of toy is that?" Gabby asked him.

"It's a hacky sack," Adam told her. "The goal is to not let it touch the ground, but you can only kick it with your feet. It's tricky! My buddy Evan here accidentally kicked it too far."

"Sorry," said the little boy, looking at the ground. Adam put a protective hand on his shoulder. "What are you drawing?"

"It's a unicorn," Gabby said.

"A unicorn?" I asked, surprised. "I thought it was a pony. Or 'maybe a horse.'"

"It's a unicorn," she said decidedly.

"It's definitely a unicorn," Adam said, winking at me.

"Can't you see that, Cara? I think— no, I *know*— that that's the best unicorn I've ever seen."

"Thank you," Gabby said. "What's your name?"

"Adam Beck. What's yours?"

"Gabrielle Moore," Gabby told him seriously.

"Well, it is a pleasure to meet you, Gabrielle Moore," said Adam, bowing slightly. "I'm friends with your big sis Cara."

"Friends, are we?" I said. He shrugged.

"I'm friends with Cara, too," Gabby said quickly. "We're drawing."

"I see that," Adam said. "Well, we'll let you ladies get back to your fun. Evan and I will probably play some more hacky sack, but they're starting to do group activities, so we might join up with the others later. You two should come!"

"Group activities?" I frowned.

"Yeah," Adam said, pointing back towards the gazebo. "They're getting ready to start the three-legged race."

I could see teenagers standing, wobbling, with their siblings comically latched at the leg. I was already sweating from sitting out in the sun, but I suddenly felt even sweatier.

"No one told me anything about group activities."

"Chill. No one's forcing you to join in," Adam said. "But it would be fun if you did."

"Maybe later," I said. "We have unicorns to draw."

Adam flipped the hacky sack into the air, then caught it on the toe of his sneaker. "Good luck with that." He kicked the ball towards Evan, who kicked it straight up. Adam reached out with his hand and snatched it from midair.

"You broke the rules," Gabby said.

"I lose," Adam admitted. "Well, we're going to go play over there in the shade. Maybe we'll see you later?"

"Maybe," I said, waving him off. He took the hint and ran back to the gazebo with Evan.

As the afternoon wore on, a few counselors came by to bring us water bottles and encourage us to join the group activities, but fortunately for me, Gabby was engrossed with her drawings. We waited out the three-legged race, a hula hoop contest with multiple rounds (as they only had three hula hoops), a ball-throwing contest, a water balloon toss, and a few laps around a couple of trees before Gabby finally pulled at my sleeve with a chalk-covered hand.

"Can we go play with everybody else?" she asked. She had a streak of pink powder across one of her cheeks, like war paint. I brushed the chalk dust from my hands and cleared my throat.

"Sure," I said, not sure at all. We scooped up the pieces of chalk that had rolled away from us and headed back to the gazebo, where I returned the box to one of Isa's canvas bags.

"Can we do the next game?" Gabby asked. I hesitated.

"Yeah. Maybe just that one game." I spotted Sebastian standing out in the grass with a clipboard. I swallowed hard and walked up to him.

"Hi. Sebastian?"

"Hello there," he said pleasantly. His over-large glasses, impressive belly, and friendly tone gave him a surprisingly approachable air, even though he towered over me. I instantly felt somewhat at ease.

"I'm Cara," I said. "I'm on your calling list."

"Nice to meet you, Cara."

"Nice to meet you, too."

"Are you looking for Audie? Because of that stuff I said on the phone?" Sebastian looked worried. "I'm really sorry about that. It didn't sound like something I should have gotten involved in."

"No, that's no problem," I said, realizing that I still hadn't seen Ms. Wells. "I was just wondering... what do I have to do to get into the next game or whatever?"

"Nothing, except participate," he said. "We're doing a wheelbarrow race next. Just go stand by that tree. We're using it for a starting line."

"Wheelbarrow race?" I choked.

"Yeah, you know, your little sister will walk on her hands, and you'll hold her feet and kind of keep her balance."

"Yeah, I know how it works." God, how'd I end up in the wheelbarrow race? And yet there was Gabby, bouncing up and down and grinning like a maniac at the thought of being a wheelbarrow, so I shepherded her over to the pine tree where about fifteen other sibling duos were waiting. I didn't recognize any of them except Adam and Evan, who were hacky sacking off to the side. Evan kicked it high again, but Adam caught it and tucked it into his pocket before they lined up with the other groups.

"Can you believe all this crap?"

The voice was familiar. I turned around to find Chase lounging against the trunk of the pine tree, arms folded like a pretzel. My heart skipped just a little. I was very, very aware of how much I probably smelled from being outside for so long.

"Believe what?"

"This Summer Siblings stuff," he smirked, gesturing to everything around us. "Year after year. It's just kind of dumb."

"If it's crap... why do you do it?" I asked.

He shrugged, then pointed at Isa, who was directing teenagers and kids into a straight line. "Look how into it she is. Way too extreme."

I thought about calling him out on the subject change, but considering I was queen of the question dodge, I let it go. "I guess it's just her thing."

"It's weird."

"Maybe," I said. "I didn't even know you were here."

"Yeah, we got here late, and we've been doing these group things the whole time. Letting Isa boss us around…"

"Where's your, um, little brother?"

"He's over there," Chase pointed to a skinny little boy who was busy tearing up fistfuls of grass. "Derek. He just never stops, you know? Always wants to do something."

"Same with Gabby," I agreed. "She's just this little ball of energy."

"Yeah. It's whatever, though. I heard Mrs. Jameson is going to be bringing pizza for everyone."

"That's, uh, a lot of pizza," I said moronically.

The dust settled around our conversation. Our commonality ended at pizza.

"Okay, everyone spread out!" Isa yelled at the top of her thin voice. She looked like she was in desperate need of a megaphone. Nina sat cross-legged in the grass behind her, while Sebastian and another counselor stood nearby, watching Isa with amused smiles the way adults watch a toddler.

I took Gabby's hand and moved away from Chase. "Can you do a handstand, Gabby?"

"No," she said, her eyebrows tilting up in concern.

"It's okay, it's okay," I said quickly. "You know what? That's actually good, because you don't need to do a full handstand at all. You'll stand on your hands, but I'll hold your feet for you so you won't fall over. Then you walk, but you walk on your hands instead of your feet."

"I don't know if I could balance."

"I bet you could," I countered. "For pizza?"

"I'll do anything for pizza!" said Gabby earnestly. It sounded exactly like something Aaron would have said, with equal sincerity. My heart felt sore, like it was bruised, and I couldn't help but poke at it, just to see the depth of the hurt.

Gabby thrust her hands into the grass and kicked her feet up in the air, flailing and spastic. I grabbed her feet as they kicked uselessly and lifted her legs so that she was almost upside down.

"Am I doing it? Am I a wheelbarrow?"

"You're the best wheelbarrow here!" I said, channeling my inner Isa. "Now, all you have to do is move your hands like they're your feet."

I thought her wobbly little twig arms would give out, but she had some power in them. Running behind her, watching her tear through the grass, I thought "lawn mower" might have been a more appropriate moniker. I had to hunch over uncomfortably so that I wouldn't lose my grip on her ankles, but she seemed so upside downedly happy that I didn't really mind. We wheelbarrowed our way back to the starting line, next to our competitors.

"Everyone ready? Okay, the finish line is that row of bushes. Everyone see it? Yes? Okay! On your mark... get set... go!" shouted Isa.

"Come on, Gabby!" I yelled, surprised at the words that burst from me, shocked by my own volume. Her little biceps pumped fiercely as we pushed forward. I tried not to go overly fast so that she wouldn't get caught up under her own arms, but she didn't seem to have any other speed except *shooting bullet*. I didn't know the kids racing next to us, but they seemed to be slightly more in sync. But for what we lacked in gracefulness, Gabby made up for in sheer determination.

"Keep going!" I cried, and Gabby's arms churned harder. We managed to overtake the duo on our right, but I could see others pulling away and beating us to the finish line. When we finally crossed, Gabby's arms collapsed beneath her. I dropped down, too. We lay on our backs, staring up into the deep cerulean sky, while we caught our breaths until we were breathing in unison.

"Did—we—win?" she panted.

"No, I don't think we won, but you did so good, Gabby!" I said, grinning. "You were great!"

"We didn't win?"

"We beat some people," I told her. I really had no idea what place we'd finished in.

"Can we still get pizza?"

"Of course. Pizza, win or lose."

I turned my head to look at her. She smiled happily up at the sky.

"That cloud looks like a pepperoni," she said, pointing up at a cloud that was vaguely circular in shape.

"Do you like pepperonis?"

"I looove pepperonis!"

A figure appeared standing over us, blocking the sun. I squinted, trying to see the silhouette.

"Good game, ladies." It was Adam, his voice deep and friendly, his eyes smiling, his hand extended.

"Thanks," I said. I reached up to shake his hand, but he grabbed hold and pulled me up into a sitting position, then sat down beside me. Evan plopped down next to Adam.

"We won," Evan announced, looking at me for a reaction.

"Oh yeah? Good job," I told him. "Say congratulations, Gabby."

She sat herself up and looked at Evan. "Did you cheat?"

Adam laughed. "No, we didn't cheat. Evan and I have been buddies for a very long time, and we like playing games like this."

Gabby accepted that. She looked at Evan and said seriously, "Good job on winning."

"Thanks." Then, in the whiplash manner that only children can speak, "Wanna go meet one of my best friends?"

"Can I go, Cara?" Gabby asked me.

"Sure."

Evan and Gabby left for the gazebo, where several kids had gathered for the shade it provided. I watched her go, picking idly at blades of grass, unsure I wanted to talk with Adam any further.

"So I heard that you're not going to college," he said. It didn't sound mean or unfriendly, but I bristled.

"Wow. That came out of nowhere."

"Sorry. Just making conversation."

"Well, so what? Not everyone *has* to go to college, you know."

"I know, I know," he said, holding up his hands playfully, like he was warding off an attack from me. "Like I said... just asking. I always got the impression that you really liked school, though. You were really smart. I always pegged you as a college girl."

"You didn't even really talk to me in school," I pointed out. "And you're talking about me like we graduated five years ago, not a month."

"Sorry," he said lightly. "But what are your plans, then? If you're not going to college?"

I frowned up at the endless blue above us. The relentless sun made me want to snap, but I took a deep breath and simply spread my arms out, empty and wide. "Nothing."

"Nothing," Adam repeated. "Wow. Interesting girl, Cara Carson. Loves school, says no to college. Has her whole life ahead of her, but not a single plan."

I swatted at a lonely ant that was crawling up my leg. "I don't see how this is any of your concern."

"You're right."

"You're really starting to annoy me," I said, pointblank.

"Sooorrrry," Adam enunciated, stretching the syllables. "I'm not a bad guy, Cara. I'm just trying to talk to you."

"You didn't talk to me in school," I repeated.

"For which I apologize," he said. "I seem to be apologizing a lot to you."

"What's your deal, anyway? Did Mrs. Jameson ask you to keep an eye on me or something? Did Isa ask you to make sure I play nice with the others? Did Aud— did one of the counselors tell you to get me more involved?"

"Nope. God, Cara. When's the last time you let yourself have a real friend?"

I didn't look at him. My fingers pushed past the grass roots and found dirt.

"I'm not going to apologize for that one," Adam told me. "And since I've already apologized to you at least three times in the last three minutes, how about we call it a draw?"

His easy and honest way of talking bothered me and made me especially aware of my own inability to do so. I wished he would go away.

"Alright then," Adam said when I didn't answer, as if reading my thoughts. He stood up and walked over to where Evan was kicking a tree with Derek, Chase, and a few other kids. There was no doubt in my mind that Chase had probably started the tree kicking. Gabby was standing back a little, watching.

All of a sudden, kids and teenagers starting flooding the gazebo, coming at it from all directions. I stood up to see Mrs. Jameson walking towards everyone, carrying a stack of pizza boxes in her arms. And behind her, tall and thin and with pizza boxes up to her chin, strode Audie Wells.

"Pizza time!" Isa yelled from the gazebo. Other counselors called out the same, beckoning everyone to gather. The few stragglers who had not run over immediately made their way in. Gabby came running back across the field towards me.

"Pizza, pizza, pizza, pizza!" she yelled, tugging at my hand as hard as she could. "Hurry, Cara, they said we can only have one piece each!"

"I'm coming, I'm coming" I said. I was touched that she left the gazebo to come get me. The smell of cheese and bread wafted over. I allowed myself to be pulled in, by the smell, by the breeze, by Gabby— my friend.

CHAPTER 7

I dropped Gabby off at her house later that evening. She yelled goodbye to me as she ran up the path and let herself in through the front door, which was, again, unlocked. I kept the car running in the driveway an extra moment before leaving. Sooner or later, I was going to have to go in.

Later, I decided.

"Mom, I'm home," I called as I entered my own house. Something smelled delicious, but the three slices of pizza— Mrs. Jameson had ordered way too much and we all got extra— were sitting solidly in my stomach.

"We're in the kitchen," Mom called back. *We?* My heart dropped. I walked briskly to the kitchen to find my mother and father sitting at the table together. My parents had been divorced for years, long before Aaron died. After his death, my parents, awkward but cordial, agreed to have dinner with me, together, once a month, trying to salvage what was left of our broken little family. It was always an uncomfortable dinner for everyone, all of us trying to pretend that we were puzzle pieces that neatly fit together for a couple of hours.

"Hello, Cara," Dad said, nodding at me as I stood there. "It's good to see you." I gave him a small smile. My dad had always been a good guy, though difficult to read and oftentimes distant. His eyes could cloud over at a moment's notice, and then he would be gone. I should probably mention that hereditariness to Ms. Wells.

"We're having baked chicken tonight," said Mom. I wondered what she and Dad had been talking about before I came home. "We've been waiting for you."

"I actually already ate," I said. "With my little sister and the rest of the, uh, group."

"You already ate?"

"Your little sister?"

"No, I haven't already eaten my little sister," I said, attempting a joke. Neither of my parents smiled. Dad looked to Mom in complete confusion.

"Cara, why would you eat when you knew we were having dinner tonight?" Mom asked.

"I forgot. And I told you we were going to the park today," I said, hovering near the kitchen door, ready to put an end to this non-conversation and lock myself in my room. I had talked to people all day. I needed a break.

"You didn't tell me anything," she replied calmly. "You yelled something about getting Gabby as you ran out the door."

"Oh." At least I had the grace to feel a little ashamed. "Sorry."

"What little sister?" Dad asked again. I stayed silent. Mom pulled a chair out from the table and patted the seat.

"Cara, why don't you come sit down and tell us about

your volunteer work while we have dinner?" It wasn't a question.

"Mom, I just told you that I already ate. I'm not hungry. I'm not going to eat a second dinner."

"Then come sit with us while we eat. Your father drove all the way out here to have dinner with you, and we're both hungry."

I grimaced, but sat stiffly in the chair next to my mother. My father faced us with his dark hair, thinner than mine, but close in color. His eyes were tired, but they weren't closed off just yet. Family life had never seemed to suit him, like a poorly sized piece of clothing in which he could never sit comfortably.

"What's this little sister you mentioned?" he asked, a third time. I looked to my mother for help. "Will one of you please explain to me about this sister?"

"Cara signed up to… be part of a group that works with underprivileged children. She's been assigned a little sister," Mom said, mercifully leaving out the part that the "group" was a summer camp and that my therapist had been the catalyst.

"Well, that's great, Cara," my dad said, heaving a smile onto his lined face. "I like hearing that you're doing something." Mom stood up and made for the oven, where she pulled out a whole chicken. A steaming bowl of broccoli was already on the counter. Dad didn't seem to have anything more to add, so I got up and grabbed plates and silverware, setting them on the table with a clatter.

"Can you get me a lemonade while you're up, Cara?" Dad called from his seat. "If you have any?" My ears were burning, but I stuck my head in the fridge to cool them down and made his drink anyway, filling a glass with water for myself. I cracked ice into the glasses, watching fissures snake through the cubes. Mom bustled around by the stove for a little longer than she probably needed to. We both sat back down at the table at the same time.

"What shall we toast to?" she asked, holding up her drink. They did this at every Family Dinner—toasted to something, almost always to me. Once, in desperation for something positive, they toasted to my grade point average.

"To Cara," said Dad, predictably. "And to her dedication to volunteer work and charity, and all that comes with it."

"To siblings," I added quietly, the first time I had ever voiced anything during the toast. Mom glanced at me, but said nothing. We clinked glasses. I put mine to my mouth, wetting my lips, but didn't take much more than a tiny sip. My parents directed their full attention to the food on their plates. I studied the grain of the table as if I had never seen it before.

"The chicken is great, May," my father said after a while.

"Thank you. I left out the rosemary this time, since Cara doesn't care for it."

I swirled the ice around in my glass and ignored the comment. Our dinners were usually short on small talk, but this was a new level of quiet. I couldn't help but notice that he had used the exact same adjective to describe my volunteering as he did my mother's chicken.

I wished I could have said that thought aloud, or said anything, to break the frozen tundra of our family life, but I didn't. My parents ate in mostly silence, making an occasional comment about the food or the benefits of volunteering. I sipped at my water. When both of their plates were finally empty, I brought them to the sink, to give them some time to speak in case they wanted to talk about me. But still, neither said anything beyond Mom commenting on what a hot summer it had been so far. The swan song of all dying conversations.

After a long, quiet minute, my dad pushed away from the table and walked over to me. He gave my cheek a quick kiss.

"Glad I got to see you, Cara," he said. "Your mother and I are very proud of you."

"Thanks," I responded neutrally. "Bye, Dad."

"Okay. See you next month," he said. "Goodbye, May."

"Bye, Dennis. Until next month," Mom replied. She waited until he left, letting himself out through the front door. We listened to his car engine roar, then fade away. Then she turned to me. "You could have been a little friendlier."

"Me?" I said incredulously. "Mom, you barely said anything yourself."

"He doesn't do it for me, Cara. I don't do it for him. We do it for you."

"I don't need these pity dinners, Mom. We're not a family. We haven't been a family for a long time. And you and I both know that it's physically impossible for us to ever be a family again."

I immediately regretted saying it, but I turned quickly and left before my words could register and blossom into emotion on her face. I didn't want to see her any more broken than she already was. She had already lost one child. I didn't need to see her feeling like she was losing another.

The window in my bedroom faced east, which meant I never got to watch the sunset, but I did get to witness the sky change colors, the sun pouring its last light over our house until the dredges turned dark and the stars glinted through. Tonight's show was a calm and milky sort of pink, desperate to be orange, a shade away.

I wanted to go to sleep, to put the day to bed, but I was restless. I pulled out my laptop and read through a dozen pointless, poorly edited online articles, skipping through the clickbait, before noticing that I had an email in my inbox.

Hi Cara! I hope you had a great time at your first Summer Siblings event. I'm sorry I didn't get a chance to talk with you. Sebastian told me you had been looking for me. I spotted you while everyone was eating, but I didn't want to disturb your time with Gabby. Remember, you can call and set up an appointment for any time if you need to.
Wishing you the best,
Audie Wells

I moved the mouse around on the screen thoughtfully, tracing an invisible figure eight. Ms. Wells didn't often email me. When she did, it was usually just a reminder to make a new appointment.

I clicked *Reply*, but couldn't think of anything to type. I deleted her email, closed my laptop, and crawled under my quilt, even though I was wider awake than ever. With nothing better to do, I pulled out my green journal.

One SS event down, and I still miss Aaron just as much. It's ridiculous to expect to feel any differently so soon, but I thought maybe there would be... something. I don't know. Every time I open this journal, I think about how great it would be to write about a huge breakthrough or radical shift, but so far I'm the same small, petty person who's rude to her mother and blaming her grief for all her shortcomings. Maybe I'll be a better sister than a daughter. I can only hope.

I called Gabby the next day, just to see how she was doing, and in return, she called me daily for the next week, just to chatter. She described each of her stuffed animals in vivid detail and recounted adventures and fights with her little brother, Logan. She took the phone outside and counted the number of bugs she saw. She reminded me of our own pizza and ice cream stories multiple times.

"Hey, Cara, remember when we ate pizza at the park? Outside?"

"Yeah, I remember."

"We didn't even have plates!"

"I know. It was pretty crazy."

Sometimes her enthusiasm reminded me of a young Aaron, and that hurt. That was when I would have to tilt the phone away from my face and control my breathing, blinking hard and deliberately. But sometimes, she did or said something entirely new, of her own little personality, that made me stop and smile. I found myself looking forward to her daily calls.

"Hey, Gabs," I said when my phone rang late one evening.

"Cara?"

That was definitely not Gabby on the line. "Hello?"

"Cara, it's Sebastian."

"Oh, shoot," I said out loud. Why couldn't he just email me? Why hadn't I bothered to look at the name on the screen? "Sorry, Sebastian. I thought you were someone else."

"No big deal!" Sebastian laughed. "Listen, I'm just calling to remind you about the next Summer Siblings trip to the zoo. Remember, it's this upcoming Friday."

It was already on my calendar. "I'll check with my little sister, but I'm sure we'll be there."

"Okay. We're meeting there as soon as it opens at nine. It should take about three hours or so. If you need more details, call me back at this number."

"Okay."

"Alright. I have more calls to make, so I'll talk to you later."

"Bye," I said, then headed downstairs to find Mom. She looked up from the book she was reading when I entered the living room.

"In order to avoid another dinner fiasco, I'd like to officially inform you that I will be taking Gabby to the zoo this Friday," I said curtly.

"This Friday?"

"Yes."

"I think you have a dentist appointment, Cara."

"What?"

"I think so. Go check the calendar."

I ran to the kitchen to check our big calendar, which hung on the fridge. I found "CC— Dentist, 11 AM" written in my mother's handwriting on Friday's square.

"No!" I protested. "Mom, you *work* for the dentist, can't you change my appointment?"

"No, Cara, I made that appointment for you five months ago."

"Seriously? I have to miss a Summer Siblings event for an appointment at the place where my mother controls the appointments?"

Mom put her book down on the arm of her chair. "Cara, I'm pleased to hear you so focused on the Summer Siblings, but we cannot change your appointment. I'm glad you're doing something with your time, but you still have a responsibility to keep your previous commitments."

"I'm not going."

"You're going, end of discussion. Your dental hygiene is very important."

"Oh, my God! Can you hear yourself? That is literally the stupidest thing I've ever heard," I said passionately.

We both heard the whine in my voice. Mom offered me a smile.

"Do you hear *yourself*? You sound like a teenager," she informed me.

"Yeah, well, I *am* a teenager," I grumbled.

"Why don't you invite Gabrielle over for that evening instead?" Mom suggested.

"What, like, to eat with us? We don't exactly have a great handle on dinners."

"Maybe she'd be interested in spending the night. I think that would be cute."

"Cute," I repeated. Mom tapped a finger against her book. "I guess she might like that."

"You loved spending the night out when you were young," Mom told me.

"Probably to get away from you," I said sarcastically,

smiling at her.

"I think it's a good idea," Mom said. "It'll be fun. I can dig around in the attic and find some old toys."

"*Okay,*" I said, trying to stress that the conversation was over. Mom smirked slightly behind her book as I made my way back upstairs, already dialing Gabby's house phone on my cell. She answered at the first ring.

"Gabby." I felt weirdly nervous. "Your mom might have told you that we were supposed to go to the zoo with the Summer Siblings on Friday, but for reasons beyond my control, I'm not going to be able to take you. Do you want to come over to my house on Friday evening instead?"

"What's at your house?"

"Oh, I don't know. We could find fun stuff to do. And you could spend the night if you wanted."

"A sleepover!"

"Exactly," I said, and then added, "but you have to ask your mom first."

"She says it's okay," Gabby said immediately.

"Gabby," I said sternly, but I was grinning. "I know you didn't ask her. You didn't leave the phone."

She paused for a few seconds, during which I could hear her breathing. "I just asked. She said it's okay."

"No, Gabby. I know you didn't ask."

"I promise she'll say it's okay! I don't hafta ask."

"Can I talk to her? Can you get her on the phone right now?"

"She's sleeping."

I chewed on my lip for a moment. "Okay, I'm going to come over on Friday and make sure it's okay for you to stay at my house. Deal?"

"Deal," she said.

"Bye, Gabs."

"Bye, Cara! See you Friday."

I made the drive out to Gabby's house that Friday afternoon, leaving my mom to dig through our old Disney movies and toys. As the week had gone on, her excitement grew, and if I had to admit it, so did mine. And it was kind of nice to see Mom enthusiastic, especially about something that I was excited for, too.

When I pulled into the driveway, I sat in my car as usual, then realized that Gabby would not be barreling through the door like she normally did. I was supposed to go in to speak to her mother, and then hopefully, take Gabby back with me. I took my time fixing my hair in the mirror on my sun visor before meandering my way around puddles up the front path to the door. A late afternoon thunderstorm had drenched their neighborhood, leaving water dripping from their gutters onto my head. I knew the door wasn't locked, but I knocked politely anyway.

I could hear pounding footsteps and a small scuffle on the other side; when the door finally opened, Gabby beamed up at me, one hand holding the door, the other hand keeping a toddler slightly at bay.

"Cara's here!" she screamed, her huge, toothy smile in place. "Cara's here, Cara's h—Logan, get *off*." She let go of the door to push her little brother. I stepped in quickly, pulled the door closed behind me, and knelt down.

"Hi, Logan. I'm Cara," I said. The boy wore just a diaper and a green-striped shirt, barefoot and sucking on two of his fingers. He stared at me and blinked a few times, then looked away bashfully. "Gabby, where's your mom?"

"In here." She pointed down a hallway, where I could see an entrance to another room, dark, with a flickering light. I steeled myself and headed to the doorway.

"Mrs. Moore?" I asked, feeling very uncomfortable. A woman was lying on her side on a patterned sofa that was pushed against the wall, letting the vapid light of the television sweep over her, washing out her features. She directed her eyes towards me, but made no move to get up. The remote, a cordless phone, and a full glass of water were within arm's reach.

"Hi, I'm Cara," I said, uncertain that she would recognize just my voice from our brief phone conversations. "I'm your daughter's... well, we... I work with, um, play with your daughter through the Summer Siblings. With Mrs. Jameson? Earla?"

The woman continued to look at me, then nodded. I moved further into the room but felt horribly exposed. I glanced around, taking in the colorful curtains, the bright pillows, all the homey furnishings. The décor did not add up to the broken and drained woman on the couch.

"I was hoping to get your permission to have Gabby sleep over at my house tonight," I said, twisting my hands together. "I'd bring her back home tomorrow morning, of course, whenever she wakes up."

"That's fine."

"Are—are you sure?" I asked, a little bothered, but not sure why. "I mean, you don't even know me." The words left before I could stop them. Great way to convince her to send her daughter with me overnight.

"Gabby knows you."

"Right, I mean, there's no reason that you shouldn't, but…" I bit at my lip. "But, Mrs. Moore, do you…"

I couldn't think of how to finish my sentence. *Do you want to know anything about me? Do you want to meet my mom?* Mrs. Moore's eyes drifted back to the television.

"Okay, well, thanks for trusting me, I guess. I'll just get Gabby's sleeping bag for her, and then we'll be on our way."

A short pause.

"She doesn't have a sleeping bag."

"Oh." I remained standing in the open floor, feeling like an empty raft adrift at sea. "Well, I'm sure we can find something at my house for her to sleep on. She can have my bed. I'll sleep on the floor."

Mrs. Moore's entire attention seemed to be back on the television. It was on mute, with an infomercial full of clean-cut women with enormous white teeth holding up gaudy jewelry. I glanced at it, watching their mouths move soundlessly, watching the numbers and words scrolling across the bottom of the screen, and for a moment, I would have liked very much to have curled up on the carpeted floor and let the day go by with Mrs. Moore, not thinking about anything. With effort, I tore my gaze away from the screen and back to the sad woman on the sofa. I desperately wanted to say something to her, but I didn't know what. A distant clock ticked from somewhere in the house.

Mercifully, Gabby came running into the room, Logan on her heels.

"Momma! He won't leave me alone!"

"Momma! Momma!" Logan wailed in turn. Mrs. Moore curled up a corner of her lips in a small smile and reached out an arm, to which he clung. It was difficult to see in the dim room, but I thought her eyes were full of tears.

"Say bye, Gabby," I said, feeling increasingly weird about my sudden sense of authority. Seeing how tenderly she held Logan, I almost didn't want to take Gabby from Mrs. Moore. "Sleepover time."

"Bye, Momma!" said Gabby. She bent over her mother and planted a sloppy but loving kiss on her cheek.

"Bye, baby," said Mrs. Moore, who managed to sit up just a bit to kiss Gabrielle back. Then Gabby ran from the room, and I found myself with just Mrs. Moore and Logan, who was no longer crying but watching the silent television with his mother.

"Well, like I said, I'll bring her back tomorrow morning. Thanks again, Mrs. Moore," I said, edging towards the hall.

She lifted her eyes to my face one final time, the effort seeming to cost her. She called in the general direction of her daughter, "Be good for Cara, Gabrielle."

"I will!" came Gabby's voice. She was in the hall, tugging a dark blue, beat up duffel bag. The zipper was only partially closed. I peeked inside; there seemed to be six different outfits in there, all varying shades of pink. I pulled the zipper all the way shut before hoisting the bag onto my shoulder.

"Goodbye, Mrs. Moore. Thank you."

"Bye, Momma! I love you!" Gabby ran out the door before waiting to hear a response.

"I love you, too," Mrs. Moore said, even though her daughter was already gone. I stayed behind for an extra minute, trying to think of something more to say. Was this how I was supposed to help Gabby? Was this where I could inflict change, in her life and in mine?

If that had been my opportunity, I ungraciously let it pass me by. I just couldn't do it. Couldn't think of anything to say, couldn't think of anything to do. I couldn't be the kind of sister I truly wanted to be.

CHAPTER 8

"Is this your house?" Gabby asked as we pulled up in my driveway.

"Yep."

She ran up the front path to the door, which my mother flung open, as if she had been anticipating us since the moment I left. I took my time collecting Gabby's duffel bag from the trunk.

"Are you Cara's mom?" asked Gabby.

"Yes, I am. My name is Ms. May. And you must be Gabrielle!" said Mom.

"Miss-may-miss-may-miss-may!" chanted Gabby, beaming. She sidestepped Mom and ran into our house. Mom offered to take the bag from me, but I shook my head and climbed the stairs to my room, where I deposited it on the floor. My room was tidy; books were stacked as neatly as they would ever be, clothes were shut away in their dresser drawers, and my bed was neatly made, for the first time in ages. Downstairs, Mom and Gabby were already tearing into

Mom's first activity of the afternoon— baking cookies from scratch. Mom handed Gabby a spoonful of raw cookie dough.

"Don't tell your mother," Mom instructed Gabby. Then she handed me a spoon, stage whispering, "Don't tell *your* mother, either." She laughed like it was the funniest thing in the world.

"I won't," I said conspiratorially, then made a show of turning around to eat the dough. My mother doubled over and clutched at her sides, hooting with laughter. It had been a long time since I had done anything to make her laugh. When Mom wasn't looking, I tipped the bag of chocolate chips into the bowl and watched the morsels pile up.

With the cookies in the oven, Mom settled down at the kitchen table with a magazine, a cow timer at her elbow that would moo when the cookies were ready. Our living room looked like a partial page from my childhood. She had pulled out board games, my old dollhouse, a chipped and cracked tea set, picture books with faded covers, and some of my old dress up costumes. I noticed that none of Aaron's old toys were out.

"Let's play dollhouse," Gabby said to me. We left Mom to her reading while we knelt before the old wooden house. Most girls had plastic dolls with stiff hair and elbows that didn't bend, but I had four soft cloth dolls that Mom had made and stuffed with cotton. They couldn't stand like the plastic dolls, but they were very huggable. Gabby picked up all of them, pressing them to her face.

"I like these dolls," she told me. "But you should have more."

"Sorry. My mom made one for each member of our family. That one's her, May; that one's my dad, Dennis. That one's me, and this one—" I took the doll gently from her— "is my brother. Aaron. I told you about him, remember?"

Gabby placed the Cara doll and the May doll in one of the rooms, propping them up against the walls. But she clutched the Dennis doll tightly.

"This is your dad?"

"Well, it's just the father doll in general, I guess."

She stared at it.

"Gabby?"

She looked up at me, tears streaming down her smooth cheeks, tracing dark paths on her face. She suddenly looked old for only seven years on this earth.

"I miss my daddy," she said, and in an instant, she was curling up against me, pressing into the contour of my body, her elbow in my stomach and her head jutting under my chin. "I want him to come home."

My arms wrapped around her tiny body. I rocked back and forth a couple of times, but it felt unnatural, so I just held her and let her cry into the fleshy part between my shoulder and chest. Her sobs grew; her breath shortened and her nose ran.

"I— don't— know— where— he— is—"

"He... he still loves you, Gabby," I said, hoping I wasn't inadvertently telling a lie.

"He doesn't love Momma. He wouldn't've left if he loved her."

I didn't have an answer to that, so I just held her. She finally drew a shuddering breath, and her shoulders stopped shaking.

"Do you... do you think about your dad a lot, Gabby?"

She nodded.

"Do you cry every time?"

She shrugged. "The sadness just won't get out."

"It's okay," I told her. "I cry about my brother a lot."

She didn't answer, but snuggled up against me as if I were enough.

I would never be enough, but I didn't have the heart to break that image of me. I held Gabby even tighter.

"The cow is mooing! The cookies are—" Mom walked in, then halted. I looked up at her, Gabby as feeble in my arms as the dolls.

"You know what? I think I'll go get dinner. We'll have an early supper," Mom said. I shook my head, trying to indicate that I was at a loss; I needed her help. She gave me a broken smile, her eyes full.

"I'll be right back." With that, Mom slipped out the door, leaving us alone. I awkwardly smoothed down Gabby's hair, which bounced back into place, then softly kissed her forehead. She suddenly scrambled up, kneeing me painfully in the thigh, and dropped a kiss onto my cheek.

"I don't want to play dollhouse anymore," she told me, sniffling but not crying.

"Good thing," I said, "because we have to go get the cookies out of the oven."

"The *chocolate chip* cookies," she reminded me. Her face was bursting with her classic grin, despite the tear tracks still on her cheeks.

"The *extra* chocolate chip cookies," I confided. She gasped.

"Can we eat them now?"

She loved so easily, Gabby. She only needed to experience something once to love it, even when her senses of love and trust were shattered. I wondered what she would be like when she was my age. I wanted to experience that, to love and trust as easily as I breathed, but I just couldn't seem to catch my breath.

After we had pulled the cookies from the oven (crisp and just a bit burnt around the edges) and eaten three apiece, Gabby crumpled her napkin and banged her hands against the table.

"I'm bored," she announced.

"Well, what would you like to do?"

She thought. "Can I see your room?"

"Sure. It's upstairs." Without hesitating, Gabby ran towards the staircase.

"What color is it?"

"You'll see it in less than a minute, crazy." I followed her to the stairs, which she clambered up on all fours. "It's to the left."

But Gabby, having raced ahead of me, had already turned right at the top of the staircase and opened the first door. I froze, four steps from the landing.

"This looks like a boy's room!" I heard her say from inside. I felt myself swaying; my arm shot out and grabbed the banister, self-preservation even when I could barely function.

I could hear her moving around, touching stuff, *touching stuff*, Gabrielle-do-not-touch-anything, my mind screamed silently, but I couldn't speak.

Her head appeared around the doorway, peeking down at me. "Cara? Is this a boy's room? It's kind of blue, like Logan's room. Remember my brother Logan?"

My throat had closed in defiance of speaking; everything ached deep within me. I couldn't make myself move; I didn't want to see inside the room. When I didn't answer, she came out and hopped down three stairs to stand on the one above me.

"Are you okay?"

"Can you please close the door, Gabby? Can you please just close the door?"

"Alright." She ran up and pulled the door shut, then ran back down to me. "Whose room is that?"

I pushed the words out. "My brother's."

"Like the brother doll? The Aaron doll?"

"Yes."

"I knew it was a boy's room." When I didn't respond, Gabby pulled on my arm, forcing my feet to stumble up the last few stairs, where I turned left on autopilot and sat heavily on my bed.

"Your brother has a nice room, for a boy," she commented. Her use of the present tense stabbed me. She approached my bookshelf and turned her head sideways, trying to read the spines. My taste in books was gluttonous: anything to find another world in which I could live that wasn't my own. "You have a lot of books! I can almost read whole chapter books, but I still like books with pictures. Can I look at one?" She didn't wait for an answer, pulling one off the shelf and thumbing through it. She soon threw it to the ground and grabbed another one. "Can you read it to me?"

My thoughts strayed out the door, down the hall, and into Aaron's room. I could feel a wall building in my head, bricks piling up and thick mortar slowing my mind. Be present. Gabby wanted to read with me. She climbed up on my bed and reached out her hand, touching my cheek gently.

"You look like my momma does," she said softly. "Are you gonna stop doing stuff?"

"What do you mean?" I asked, just as quietly. She let her hand drop from my face at my words, looking relieved that I had spoken.

"My momma is sad," she said simply.

"I can tell."

"She used to be happy, but then she got sad when the baby died. I don't think she knows how to be happy anymore. Like she forgot. She only knows how to be sad." Gabby shifted, tucking her legs underneath her. "I told her I would teach her how to be happy again, but then Daddy left, and she said she would never be happy ever again."

Little tendrils of sympathy for Mrs. Moore wound around my heart. I didn't know what to say, but I was saved by the sound of Mom shutting the front door downstairs.

"Girls, pizza's here!" Mom called up the stairs. "Who's hungry?"

Gabby flew from my bed, shrieking and crashing down the stairs. Her unwavering enthusiasm would make her an excellent cheerleader one day; her piercing voice carried all the way from the kitchen.

Downstairs, Mom was setting out paper plates and napkins. Gabby had her nose pressed up against the cardboard of a pizza box. I walked over to Mom and kissed her cheek. She turned to me, surprised, running her hand along my hair like she used to when I was very young.

"Thanks, Mom," I said, "for... doing all this. You're making Gabby really happy."

She seemed genuinely touched by my gesture. "You're making *me* really happy, Cara."

Our shadows loomed, dark watercolors, on the ceiling above us, blurry edged and undefined. Gabby had requested a nightlight, but the best I could provide was a heavy flashlight balanced on a stack of books. I had offered her my bed, but she insisted on using my flimsy old sleeping bag "like at a real sleepover," and then further insisted that I join her on the floor. I dragged my quilt off my bed and pulled a few extra blankets from my closet, making a little nest for myself next to her. Gabby, in her white pajamas with pink polka dots, clutched a worn, well-loved giraffe under one arm. It was missing half the fuzz around its scraggly neck. Under her other arm, she held a plush kangaroo, in much better condition than the giraffe.

"What're their names?" I asked of the animals. Gabby pulled the giraffe out first and sat him up. His faded yellow neck flopped depressingly over, while his matte button eyes stared into nothingness. It was kind of cute in a really pitiful way.

"This is Giraffe," she said. "I got him from my daddy when I was born because my name started with a G, and giraffes start with G. Logan got a lion from Daddy because Logan starts with L, and lions start with L. Guess what Logan named it."

"What?"

"He calls it Logan!" Gabby giggled.

Suddenly, realization dropped into my stomach like a lead block. I immediately regretted asking, but she displayed the kangaroo without a change in expression.

"And this is Kangaroo. She was gonna belong to the baby. Daddy bought her as soon as we learned that the baby was gonna be a girl, and we were gonna name her Kourtney, because Kourtney starts with K and kangaroos start with K. But then Daddy left, and nobody was taking care of Kangaroo, so I took her."

"That was very nice of you," I said softly. I reached out and touched the kangaroo's velvety nose. "I'm sure Kangaroo loves being with you."

"Where are your stuffed animals?"

"I don't have any."

"Who do you cuddle with when you're sleepy?"

"No one," I said. It sounded so much more pathetic than I meant.

Gabby frowned. "Don't you get lonely?"

I was always lonely, but a stuffed animal wouldn't solve that, so I simply said, "Not when I'm sleeping." Truth was, sleeping was almost as good as reading, because I had no recollection of my real life during the dreams. It was only the occasional nightmares that gave reading the edge over sleeping.

"I don't believe you," she said obstinately. I laughed.

"You don't have to."

She wriggled her way out of her sleeping bag and crawled over to my little blanket nest. "Here," she said. "You can have Kangaroo." She gently put the stuffed animal by my face.

"Oh, Gabby," I said, leaning up on an elbow. "I could never take Kangaroo from you." I tried to hand the animal back to her. "This is from your dad."

"Yeah, but it wasn't for me," she said, firmly tucking the toy under a blanket next to me. "It was for my sister."

If I were to take a step back and look at my life objectively at this very moment, I'd see a seven year old who was a complete stranger to me a month ago asleep on my bedroom floor and me writing this— by the light of an ancient battery flashlight trying not to wake her— not because Ms. Wells told me to, but because I'm actually interested in capturing this kind of moment. I'd classify my life as peculiar at best, completely insane at worst. Maybe this all really is insane. I never expected or asked for any of this…but I'm grateful for it all.

The next morning crept into my room, a pale sunrise filtering through the window, the shade of which I had forgotten to pull down. My eyes wandered over my room awash in the soft, early sunlight. Gabby was sleeping soundly, mouth open, Giraffe's threadbare neck pinned between her shoulder and the sleeping bag. I could hear her steady breathing over the birds chirping outside, greeting the new day's opportunities.

My stiff and knotted muscles protested against my yawning stretches. Kangaroo was a foot or so away from my blanket nest. I quickly pulled it closer to me.

Gabby stirred and frowned slightly, but her face soon relaxed back into sleepy peace. I rolled onto my back and stared at my ceiling, resisting the temptation to go snuggle in my soft and comfortable bed. I thought of how my father used to pick me up if I fell asleep on the sofa, the floor, anywhere, and carry me upstairs into my bed. I thought of Gabby's father. How could anyone leave this infectious ball of energy? I thought of her mother. How could anyone not find new hope in Gabby's always-smiling face? Even when she broke down and cried, she cried herself clean and moved on, living in each new moment, a talent I did not possess.

The light in my room grew stronger and stronger until I felt like a battery being charged by it. A loud knock on the door made Gabby's eyes fly open.

"Rise and shine, ladies!" my mother sang. "Who wants chocolate chip pancakes?"

"Me!" Gabby yelled, her voice hoarse with sleep but energetic as ever. She looked around, confused, like she had forgotten where she was, and then her eyes lit up as she remembered where she was. "Cara?"

"Gabby."

"Are we really having pancakes?"

"Hmmm." I pretended to think it over. "Why don't we go downstairs and find out?"

Gabby kicked at the sleeping bag in a frenzy, trapped until I reached over and helped untangle her legs. She wriggled out and tumbled to the door in her pajamas, yelling, "Come on, Cara!" over her shoulder. Delicious smells drifted up the stairs—pancake batter and bananas and chocolate and cinnamon. In the kitchen, my mom had four different stacks of pancakes, and she was still flipping some in a pan.

"Morning, Mom," I said, going straight for the fridge, where I found a half-gallon of chocolate milk and a bottle of orange juice, neither of which had been there yesterday. "Gabby, want some milk?"

"Good morning, sweetie," said Mom. "What kind of pancakes do you want?"

I took one banana and one cinnamon, then put a chocolate chip pancake on a plate for Gabby. Our microwave dinged, and Mom pulled out a small jug of syrup.

"Wow, warm syrup, hot pancakes..." I mused. "Special occasion, Mom? Exactly how many people are you cooking for? Did more people come over in the night?"

"Oh, I just want you girls to have a wonderful time," said Mom lightly. She took a plain pancake and half a banana that had survived being chopped into the batter and sat down next to Gabby. "Did you sleep well, Gabrielle?"

"Yeah," she said, a mangled piece of pancake already stuffed into her mouth. She tried to talk around it. "Care-uh tawksinner shleep."

"What's that, sweetie?"

Gabby chugged enormous gulps of her chocolate milk and tried again. "Cara talks in her sleep."

I stared at her while my mother chuckled. "Oh, does she? What did she say?"

"She just said 'Aaron' a buncha times."

I almost turned to look at Mom, then switched my gaze to the tabletop and tried to burn a hole through it. I could feel Mom's eyes on me.

"Cara? You haven't done that since right after he..." Mom lowered her voice. "After he passed." I didn't answer.

"Can I have another pancake?" Gabby interrupted.

"Finish the one on your plate," Mom said automatically, without taking her eyes off me. Gabby looked at her syrup-soaked flapjack and poked it mournfully with her fork.

"Cara? Do you want me to call Ms. Wells?"

"No. I do not need to talk to Ms. Wells about this," I said, frowning and shoving my plate away from me. "It was a fluke, Mom. Gabby just op—" Gabby looked up at me from her plate. I carefully chose my words. "The door to Aaron's room was accidentally opened last night."

Mom glanced over at Gabby. "Oh. I see."

"Yeah. And it was just, I wasn't expecting it, okay? It was

kind of a surprise, and not the good kind. I'm not spiraling downwards or regressing or anything. It was just an accident on—someone's—part. It must have crept into my subconscious last night. I'm sorry. I can't exactly control what I do or do not dream about. I don't even remember my dream."

"There's nothing to apologize for, Cara," Mom said, putting her hand on my shoulder. I pulled away and dragged the tines of my fork through the syrup on my plate.

"Did I do something bad?" Gabby asked, looking from Mom to me and back with big, round eyes.

"No, sweetie," Mom said, turning and smiling at her. Gabby accepted that without question and went back to her soggy breakfast.

"How's your pancake?" Mom asked.

"So good!" Gabby said. "Deee-licious!"

"Cara? How are yours?"

"I'm not hungry," I mumbled. I knew it was silly, but I was embarrassed.

Mom threw her hands up in the air. "Why do I even try?" She took a bite of banana and tossed it back down on her plate. A second later, she straightened her shoulders and turned to Gabby. "Gabby, can I get you anything else?"

"More pancakes!"

I wished that I could brush off mistakes and sadness as easily as Gabby could. I wished that I didn't feel handcuffed to my grief and loneliness, a prisoner inside my mind, unable to escape from myself or that which plagued me. I wished for so much but did nothing to reach those dreams, while Gabby climbed ladders and mountains and grabbed at the clouds high above her head, refusing to let them escape through her fingers. She shone and sparkled past her past, and I wallowed and was swallowed whole by mine.

It was time for me to take some action. I just didn't know what that action was supposed to be.

CHAPTER 9

"Thank you for letting me sleep over, Cara," Gabby said politely as we idled in my car outside of her house. The noon sun was directly above us, and it was starting to get uncomfortably hot.

"You're very welcome," I replied, equally formal. She fiddled with her seatbelt. "Gabby... is something wrong?"

"No."

"I suspect otherwise."

"I don't want to go home," she said suddenly, looking up at me, pleading.

"But we're already at your house."

"I want to go back to yours."

"Why?" I asked. "Remember, my room's full of boring old books without pictures, and we didn't even have any good games."

"Your mom made real good pancakes."

"Is that it?" I asked, surprised. I knew Gabby was easily swayed by food, perhaps just as much as your average teenage boy, but I didn't think it was this big of a deal.

"And she put extra chocolate syrup in my chocolate milk. And she kissed me goodnight. And she asked me what I dreamed about. And she let me eat the pepperonis off her pizza slices."

"Oh," I said, catching on. "She gave you lots of attention."

She didn't say anything further, just looked out of the window. I tapped my fingers against the steering wheel, then said, "Let me get your bag, and I'll walk you inside." Gabby scrunched up her face but undid her seatbelt.

As always, the front door was unlocked. Gabby pushed through and immediately called, "Momma, I'm home!" There was no response, but Logan came running down the hall towards his sister.

"Gab-bee!" he sang delightedly. She hugged him and then took his hand, telling him all about her sleepover, an outpouring of words into an open, albeit disinterested, vessel. I dropped the duffel bag by the door and moved forward into the hall. A flickering of dim light on the wall told me that Mrs. Moore was exactly where I had left her yesterday afternoon, lying on the sofa, watching television.

"Mrs. Moore?" I said, entering the room with a bit more presence than I had last time. "Gabby's home. I just brought her back from my house."

"I know where she was," Mrs. Moore said. She was in the exact same clothes as the day before. "You already told me."

"I was just reminding you," I said. "I just... I think..." Words fluttered about in my mind, moth-like, but I couldn't seem to catch any of them, let alone the right ones. "Gabby had a really good time."

Mrs. Moore moved her head slightly but didn't say anything.

"And, well, she was, uh, she was just talking about a lot of stuff, and, uh, it just kind of made me think, it made me, uh, realize, that... maybe... she's not having the easiest time here. At home," I mumbled, rushing and tripping over my words, my face flushed in embarrassment.

"What are you saying?" Mrs. Moore said. Her voice suddenly had weight to it. I swallowed hard.

"Listen, Mrs. Moore..." My legs drove me forward into the room, but I felt like I was hovering over her, a disproportional giant in a room built for elves. Awkwardly, I knelt on the floor by the sofa, near her head. She looked at me strangely. I didn't blame her.

"I lost... I lost my brother three years ago," I said, gripping the sofa cushion. "In a car accident. It was... just..." Words failed me again. "I miss him so bad. Every day. It hasn't stopped hurting."

Mrs. Moore was staring at me, but I couldn't tell if she was listening or if she had shut off somewhere deep inside.

"And for me to lose a brother... well... I mean, my mom lost her son," I said. "So..."

"Gabby told you about the baby," she whispered. Her eyes welled with tears. One slipped and slid down the contour of her nose. I wanted to wipe it away.

"Yeah," I said. "And from what she's said and from what I can see... Mrs. Moore, I'm so sorry, but... isn't there anyone you can talk to about this? Someone who can get you some help? Gabby really needs you, I know it. If my mom had just stopped living her life after we lost Aaron, I never could have survived. I needed her to be strong for me, and she was, and that's the only reason I'm even able to talk to you like this right now."

"I feed my kids," Mrs. Moore said. She sat up, and our roles were suddenly reversed. I shrank under her sudden height. Her dark eyes burned through the sheen of tears, and for the first time, I felt like she was really looking at me. "I clean them. I make sure Gabby gets to school. I make sure Logan is safe here. You think... you think I don't love my kids? You think I'm not here for them? You think if I didn't love them, I could be this upset over losing my last baby? I *love* my children."

I could feel myself starting to panic. My heartbeat tripled. "I..."

"I am sorry that you lost your brother," Mrs. Moore said clearly. She looked away from me. "But you do not understand."

I couldn't respond to that. I sensed the hollowness inside of her, the cavernous emptiness that must have been left when tragedy struck, but surely she was right— comparing tragedies would get us nowhere.

"Everything's fallen apart," she added suddenly. "But you do not get to insinuate that I'm not caring for my children. You do not know what goes on in this house."

My face was on fire. I would have given anything to let the floor open up and swallow me whole, to save me from my mortification. What could I possibly say to make a graceful exit? Any exit?

An eternity passed. Mrs. Moore kept her eyes fixed on the television. I stared at the sofa cushion, frozen on my knees, wondering if I should just get up and leave without a word.

"They're great kids," I finally mumbled. "Gabby's an angel, really. She's helping me a lot. All I want... I just... I don't want to let her down."

I could hear Gabby chattering away in another room and Logan laughing. Mrs. Moore still didn't look at me. Realizing that I had been holding my breath, I let it go, then stood up and hurried from the room, head bowed. I picked up Gabby's bag in the hall and called for her; she ran up to me and grinned, pleased that I was still there.

"Where's your room?" I asked, even though everything in me wanted to leave, crawl into a hole, and never see the light of day again. "I'll bring your bag in."

She led me further down the hall to two doors across from each other. "That's Logan's room," she said, pointing to one. "And this one's mine."

She opened the door to the room on her right and flipped on the light. I walked in and stopped cold.

A tiny twin bed was pushed up against one side of the wall with a purple-and-pink striped comforter draped messily atop. Wooden letters spelling "GABBY" and painted in various shades of pink lined the wall alongside her bed. An old dresser, faded white, was against another wall next to a window, which was draped with sheer pink curtains. At the foot of her bed was a small bookshelf that came up to my hip, filled with picture books and a couple of dolls with shiny black hair. A pink-background poster of a majestic, golden unicorn was tacked just above the bed.

But it wasn't the feeling of being in a bubblegum factory that made me feel sick to my stomach. Against the other wall was a crib, decorated with lighter, pastel pinks. A butterfly mobile spun slowly over the bedding, while cutesy, cartoonish kangaroo decals stuck onto the wall at whimsical angles peered into the crib. The same type of wooden letters spelled "KOURTNEY" in a line on the wall. A changing table with drawers underneath mimicked the position of Gabby's dresser, with a brand new, infant onesie carefully folded on top.

Tightly gripping the duffel bag, unable to let go, I moved through the room to look at the tiny outfit. My left hand reached out, unbidden, and stroked the soft fabric. The pad on top of the changing table looked like it had seen better days, but the onesie was new, monogrammed with a pale pink "K" in the middle. I leaned closer to examine an inexplicable wet spot on the outfit before realizing it was from the tears dripping off of my own face.

Gabby flopped on her bed. "The baby was gonna sleep in Momma and Daddy's room until she stopped crying all night, and then she was gonna move in with me. Babies cry a lot, you know. I wouldn't mind, though. I would have loved her even if she cried forever."

I spun around, dropped the bag on Gabby's bed, and glided out of her room, feeling like my body didn't belong to me.

"Cara? Where're you going?" Gabby asked, poking her head into the hall.

"Home, Gabby," I said, trembling, already out the door. "I'll call you tomorrow."

"Cara!" she yelled, but I was already gone. Mrs. Moore was right. I had no idea what was going on inside that house.

At home, I crept past my mother dozing on the sofa and

silently made my way up the stairs. I paused at the top step and took stock of myself: relatively calm, but my feet felt as if they were glued to the stairs.

"Mooove," I whispered to myself. "Cara, move." I compelled my right foot to take a step, then my left, then right, then left, all the way to the closed door of Aaron's room. Each halting step I took felt like weights were fixed to my ankles. I rested my palms flat against the grainy wood, pressing my forehead to the door before dropping my hand down to the doorknob, not letting myself look. Twisting the handle, the door fell away from my body, and I stumbled into his room.

The shade to the window was pulled down, but I didn't dare to open it. The blue-grey walls seemed duller than I remembered. His bed was neatly made, with a folded back quilt similar to the one on my bed, though his had a different pattern and darker colors. I imagined my mother making the bed in the weeks after his death, crying as she tucked in her tears between the sheets.

I walked over to his desk and sat at the wooden chair, overwhelmed by the tiny details that were Aaron. Books and trinkets on the shelves, a couple of baseballs, a jar of coins, an old teddy bear from some girlfriend or other— all trapped in the silence of years past. Everything had a thin coat of quiet dust. With a flick of a small switch at the base, I turned on his lamp, bringing the things nearest to me into sharp focus. Like mine had, the calendar above his desk hung on October of three years ago, with the dates all crossed off up until—

Seeing that felt like a knife in my chest. I folded in half and stuck my head between my legs and tried to take deep breaths until my heart stopped pounding. Without opening my eyes, I reached up and felt around until my fingers brushed the glossy calendar page. I pulled hard, ripping away October, crumpling the page in my hand. I turned around in the chair, away from the desk, towards the open space on his floor between where I sat and his bed.

I thought about going through his closet, to see his old clothes, then realized I had just done that with Baby Kourtney's onesie. In less than a step, I made it from his desk to his bed, where I collapsed and curled up, head not even on the pillow. His quilt smelled a little musty, a little like our house. Not like him. I folded my arms around my middle and let the quilt soak up my tears, and without even trying, I fell into the most restful, peaceful sleep that I had enjoyed in a very long time.

"Oh, my God."

I jerked awake at the words, my eyes swollen and puffy. The skin on my face felt taut and tumid.

"Huh?"

"Cara, sweetie, oh my goodness." My mother was clutching at the door frame, her face pale. "I thought—"

"What?" I asked hoarsely, sitting up. My stomach growled; surely it was late in the evening. Mom walked shakily to where I was sitting and joined me on the bed.

"Oh, Cara. I didn't hear you come home. I was sleeping on the sofa. And when I woke up, I saw light in the hallway from upstairs, but it was coming from your brother's room. And, well, we haven't been in that room in so long... and when I came in and saw the door opened... and you just... you looked so much like him, when you were sleeping..."

"I'm a girl," I said bluntly, gathering and pulling my hair over my shoulder for emphasis.

THE SISTER

"I know, Cara, but you just…" Mom shrugged helplessly. "And I was still half-asleep…"

"I feel like the long hair and the boobs would have given it away."

Mom laughed, great whoops of sound that filled the room unlike the physical stuff seemed capable of doing. I arched my back and stretched. Mom reached out and caught my hand, and we sat in silence for a minute as she rubbed her thumb against mine.

"When's the last time you were in here, Mom?"

"Hm? Oh, I come by and open the door every so often. Maybe once every couple of months. But I don't… I don't actually enter the room." She looked around as if she had just realized that she had, in fact, actually entered the room. "How often do you come in?"

"Never," I confessed. "Not since right after he died." Quiet settled once again, like the dust around us.

"I miss him so much, Mom," I said, suddenly and quickly, with a pure honesty that felt like a draught of clean water. "I can't even tell you how much. I don't have the words. And I'm tired of feeling this way."

"Oh, Cara," Mom said again. She drew me into a hug, and I rested my head on her shoulder. I could hear the softness of her voice, but she wasn't crying. "I miss him so, so, so much, too. And sweetie?"

She gently pulled away while still holding onto me, so that I could see her round, tired face. "I miss you, too, Cara."

Her words struck a different kind of sadness within me. Before I could say anything, she pulled me into another hug, her hand strong against the back of my head.

"I'm sorry, Mom," I managed to say. "I didn't mean—I'm

just so sorry for everything, for how terrible I've been. I've been so awful to you, and to Dad, and Aaron never would have wanted— if he knew how I've been acting— I'm so sorry."

She didn't say it was okay, or that she forgave me, or to forget about it, because I don't think she ever really felt like I was doing her a wrong. She just held me, and for the first time, I held her, too.

"Mom?" I said finally, talking into her shoulder. "How did you... I mean, you just seemed to... I remember you being so sad, like all of us, but afterwards, you just seemed to get your life back on track. You've been so strong, especially around me, when I was nothing but horrible to you."

She let go and sat back, pensive, almost as if she wasn't quite sure of the answer herself. Finally, she said, "I just knew that there was truly nothing in this universe that I could have done to bring him back. I would have done *anything*, but there was nothing I could do. I went through my grief process, and even though I miss him every single day, drowning in my grief doesn't get me anywhere. I still had you to take care of. I still had a job to do so that I could support us. I still had a life to live, even if..."

"Even if Aaron didn't," I finished for her. The words were simultaneously acidic and bitter.

"Oh, Cara," she said sadly. "I also relied so heavily on my faith. And I had my own therapist to see, and she prescribed me anti-depressants. I still take them."

"I didn't know that," I said, surprised.

"It's true. My own strength wasn't enough at that point. It's been a long road, and I'm still walking on it."

I mulled over that for a bit. "So... if you've gotten over

your grief…"

"Oh, I don't know if I've gotten over it. It's just something that I have learned how to live with."

"Right. If that's the case…" I paused. "Why haven't we done anything to his room?"

"I don't know," she said, as another thoughtful look crossed her face. "Right after his funeral, I told myself that I would have to clean out his room, but I just couldn't face it then. I was still so wrapped up in my own pain. So I gave myself some time to heal, and told myself I would do it later, and later just escaped me."

I took a deep breath. "I think it's time we did something with it."

Mom didn't answer at first. She was gazing out the open door, at my room across the stairwell. "Where did you get that kangaroo?"

"What?" I frowned. "Did you hear me? I said I think it's time that we did something with Aaron's room, Mom. It's not helping us by just sitting up here unused and closed off."

"I see a stuffed kangaroo by your door. Was that one of Aaron's old things? I don't remember it."

"No. Gabby gave it to me. Mom, she…" I hesitated. "Her mom lost a baby last year, and the baby was going to share Gabby's room, and Gabby has to sleep in the same room with all of the stuff for the baby, and… anyway, her mom's really been struggling with it, and that's kind of why Gabby's in the Summer Siblings program."

"Poor sweetheart," Mom said, understanding lighting her eyes. I could feel her shifting her attention back to Aaron's room and my words, looking around at the walls, four slabs of gypsum and paint, nothing more. "We could certainly donate a lot of his stuff. There are countless kids out there who I'm sure would love his books. And clothes are always good things to give to charity."

"We don't have to get rid of everything," I said quickly.

"No," Mom reassured me. "We can keep some important memories. But you're right. It's not doing anyone any good sitting locked up here. It's just making us sad."

We continued to look around the room. Visions of other people, strangers, with Aaron's stuff swirled in my head. They weren't pleasant images, so I actively dismissed them, trying to be present.

"We could turn it into an office. Or a guest room. Or a crafts room," Mom suggested.

"Is this weird?" I asked quietly.

"Not having my son on this earth with me will always be weird," Mom said. "It will always be sad. It will always be painful. But having my daughter sitting next to me and talking calmly and rationally about how to move forward... is beautiful to me."

I thought about sleeping in Aaron's room tonight. Not sure why— because I got such great sleep there earlier today? Because I have something to prove? Because Gabby sleeps with all her sister's stuff? Because I'm a sociopath who doesn't relate to normal human things? Because I'm melodramatic and think I'm going to overcome something or have a better understanding of my grief if I make it through the night? Whatever the reason, I decided against it. It's not that I'm too scared or too sad— it's just that I never would have spent the night in his room without him while he was still here. There's no need to do so now that he's gone. Why start now?

Clearing out Aaron's room was difficult, to say the least. Both Mom and I wept on and off as we relived memories of him, some painful, some cathartic. Sometimes we had to brace ourselves before we could look at something; sometimes we were surprised by laughter that burst from us, unbidden but welcome. Slowly but surely, we emptied his room and moved his things into separate piles, which we then packed into cardboard boxes.

We labeled each box carefully: Goodwill for clothes, library for his books, and so on. At first, we had an enormous pile dedicated to the things we wanted to keep, the things we couldn't bear to donate, but we soon realized that that pile was bigger than the others. Breaking up the "keep" pile for more donations felt like tearing pieces of my heart away, but after nearly everything was packaged up, I realized the cuts were clean and even, not jagged and severe.

We agreed that we could each keep three things. Mom kept his quilt, folding it lovingly and smoothing out wrinkles with her slender fingers. Her hands always looked so maternal to me; everything she did with them seemed so sure and loving. She looked around his room for a while and finally said, "There's nothing else I could take that would make me feel better. I already have all his baby blankets and childhood drawings and little things that make me think of him. There's nothing else in here that's actually Aaron."

I nodded. "I'll just take one thing, too."

"That's alright, Cara. Take whatever you want."

"No," I swallowed, suddenly feeling a little guilty. "I already have... I mean, I took... I have his lucky penny keychain."

"You have it?" Mom asked, surprised. "I've been looking for it for ages! I figured you two had traded, and it was his month to have it when... I thought it was gone."

"Yeah, it was his month. But it was in the bag of his stuff that the police gave us... after," I said, tripping on the last word. "When we got it, you put it all in the closet and didn't look at it for a long time."

"I remember," Mom said.

"Well, I went in there. The day after we got it back. I had to see his stuff. I had to. I went through it all, and I took the keychain, and I put everything back. I'm sorry." The confession spilled hurriedly from me. "I'm really sorry."

"Oh, sweetie," Mom said. "You don't have to be sorry. I just wish you had told me."

"It wasn't very lucky," I whispered around the lump in my throat.

"Cara, you know that luck has nothing to do with anything."

I nodded. "There's nothing else I really want in this room. It's all a part of Aaron as a whole, but broken down, nothing really says 'Aaron' to me. I'm happy with just the keychain."

"Alright," Mom said. "I think that's just about everything. What do you think about throwing out the mattress? And donating his furniture. And we'll just... we'll get all new furnishings. A new bed, or a sofa sleeper. A fresh coat of paint. How does that sound? We'll get a new desk, and you could even come study in here, if you wanted."

"I don't have anything to study for, Mom," I reminded her. "School's out. I'm not going to college."

"Okay," she said simply, and dropped the subject. She

took my hand, and I gripped hers back tightly, and we walked out of Aaron's room without looking back.

Except I totally did look back. In fact, I went back in, late that night, while Mom was sleeping. The boxes were stacked outside of his door. I moved them around until I found the one I wanted, then carefully pulled open the flaps. The dusty old teddy bear I had spotted earlier was smushed between the side of the box and a Spanish-English school dictionary. I pulled the bear out and ruffled the dull fur, straightening the faded red bow around its neck. I stared into its once shiny, now glazed over eyes, one of which had a deep scratch across it. I had meant to give it to Gabby, as she had given me the kangaroo, but I realized I had no connection with it; even though it had belonged to Aaron, there was no sentiment attached. It was not nearly on the same level as what Gabby had given me. I already felt ashamed at the thought of giving her something just for the act of doing so. I shoved the teddy bear back into its box, packed everything away again, and retreated to my room, where Kangaroo was waiting for me on my bed—a true friend, given selflessly and in love. The teddy bear was just that: a teddy bear.

CHAPTER 10

And thus passed the first month of summer. Sebastian called again as June melted away in the southern heat, reminding me of the Summer Siblings' trip to the movies to see the latest animated film. Mrs. Jameson had rented an entire theatre for a private viewing, as there were so many of us in attendance. At the concessions, I bought the biggest tub of popcorn they had, along with peanut M&Ms and a bag of gummy bears. Gabby's code-red excitement level, simultaneously fueled by sugar, had her buzzing at high frequency. We navigated our way down the aisle, Gabby waving to everyone she saw. Audie Wells was seated in the very first row with some other counselors, but I kept my eyes averted and led Gabby towards the back of the theatre.

We squeezed ourselves into two open seats at the end of a row, and within a few minutes, the lights dimmed. I settled the popcorn on my lap, tilted towards Gabby, and tried not to think about the stickiness of the floor around my feet. Bored, I could feel my mind trying to shut down, but it was hard to stay present when I couldn't have cared less about the movie or its storyline (or lack thereof). Some happy woodland creatures found their comfortable woodland lives upturned, but through the power of love and laughter, were able to get things not just back to how they were before, but to make them *even better*. The life lessons! Oh, the life lessons, casually swirled around corny puns. I was more intrigued by Gabby's reactions. Her laugh was genuine, and her concern was deep. She gasped in total shock at the villains and cheered aloud when an obstacle was overcome. Her total absorption into the movie was incredible.

With credits rolling, Gabby clapped at the screen while she and all of the other kids celebrated the woodland creatures' success. The end of the movie signified the end of the event: lines started forming as teenagers crowded around their counselors, checking out before leaving with their siblings, which was the standard procedure at the end of all Summer Siblings activities. Gabby tried to push past my legs to the aisle, but I put a hand on her shoulder to keep her in her seat.

"Let's let everyone else leave first," I said. "So we don't have to fight the crowd."

"Why would we fight?" She struck a pose, little fists punching the air.

"It's just an expression," I said, watching the people stream through the two exits. I wasn't a big fan of crowds. Gabby directed her attention back to the big screen, trying to hum with the credits' music but missing the tune completely. A couple of theatre employees began gathering at the bottom of the stairs, holding brooms and dustpans.

"Can we go now?" Gabby asked as the majority of the

theatre emptied. The employees swarmed up into the aisles like misfit ants.

"Okay, okay," I said. Gabby picked up the half-eaten tub of popcorn, but I stopped her. "Just leave that on the floor by our seats, Gabby. They'll pick it up."

"Or you could save us a minute and throw it away yourselves, being highly competent and capable human beings having the same functioning ability as we do," said one of the employees, who was standing in the row behind me.

"What?" I turned to look and came face-to-face with Adam Beck, who was holding a broom and dustbin. "Adam. Hi. Kind of rude. But hi."

"Rude but true," he grinned, not even looking at me, but sweeping some loose popcorn into his dustbin. He was wearing the same bright red polo as the other employees.

"Don't you get paid to pick up stuff that people leave?" I asked. "Isn't that your job?"

"I get paid— minimum wage, I might add— whether you leave it or throw it away," he responded. "But wouldn't it feel nice to do a good deed and help a fellow out? Add some kindness into the world?"

Gabby nodded enthusiastically, convinced. I picked up the popcorn, irritated but feeling pressured with Gabby watching. "So you work at the movies?"

"Yep. Couldn't get my shifts changed so that I could actually watch the movie, but at least I was kind of here. Evan's hanging out with our counselor, Dawn. I actually get off after I finish cleaning up here, so I'll be able to bring him home."

"Well, you're extending your time by hanging around talking," I told him. "Bad employee."

"What do *you* do?"

I glared at him. "Nothing. Okay? I don't work."

"Then what *do* you do?" he asked, changing his emphasis.

I shifted uncomfortably. "I don't do anything. I... I hang out with Gabby."

He whistled one, low note, either in appreciation, or admiration, or sarcasm; I couldn't tell. "Well, damn. Seems like a pretty chill summer for you."

"Hey, watch it," I said, nodding towards Gabby. "Kid."

"Momma says *damn* sometimes," Gabby piped up.

"Gabby! Just because your mother says it doesn't mean you have to," I told her.

"She's right. Nice maternal instincts, by the way," Adam added casually, not in a mean tone, but in more of an offhand, joking way, like one would use among friends. Except we weren't friends.

"Why do you even work here?" I asked.

"For the glamour," he laughed. He leaned on the long handle of his dustbin and looked straight at me. "But really. Gotta earn money for college somehow."

I gestured around at the theatre. "This is gonna pay for college?"

"No," he said, chuckling. "I got three scholarships. That'll pay for the bulk of room and board fees. But I'd like to have money to spend on food and books and gas and the stuff that helps define the kind of life I'm used to living."

"Oh," I said simply, thinking of how my mother had always given me enough money for whatever I wanted to do. Then again, I hadn't wanted to do much. Just buy books and sleep. "Congratulations, I guess, on your scholarships."

"Thanks, Cara," he said, smiling broadly and kindly,

delighting in his achievements but not flaunting. "I've worked hard."

"Well," I said, reaching out and shoving the popcorn tub at his chest. He grabbed onto it reflexively. "Keep working."

I only did it to needle him, but his eyes lit up, surprised, and he chuckled genuinely; his cheerful whistling that followed me as I walked away only annoyed me. Gabby trailed after me, hopping down the steps to the exit. We checked out quickly with Sebastian, then made our way into the dimly lit theatre halls.

"Is he your boyfriend?" she asked.

"Him? Adam? No," I said firmly.

"Is he a boy who is your friend?"

"We're not really friends, Gabby."

"But you're both Summer Siblings."

I took her hand and navigated her through the people milling about in the lobby and out the cinema doors. We both blinked in the bright sunlight, having forgotten that an entire world existed outside of our enclosure. "That's about all we have in common."

"I think it's a good thing to have in common."

"It is," I agreed halfheartedly, then smiled down at her, feeling an Isa-ism coming on. "I'm just glad I'm in it because I got to meet you."

"And *I* got to meet *you!*" she cheered. I didn't mention that I thought she got the raw end of that deal.

Sebastian called the following day with another reminder. The next event for the Summer Siblings was a trip to the planetarium. The concept of space fascinated me: a place outside of time, ever expanding, full of deep mysteries and celestial secrets; nebulas, galaxies, the stuff of stars...

"You still there, Cara?"

"Yes! Yes, I am," I said quickly. I had sunk into a fantasy of the boundlessness of the universe.

"Just checking. You got pretty quiet for a while. The planetarium only has a limited number of seats, so I need to know for certain if you'll be there. We may wind up needing to go in two separate groups. Will you and your sibling be able to make it?"

I thought back to the sleepover and the flashlight. "Gabby's kind of afraid of the dark. I'll need to ask her if that's something she'd want to do before I commit."

"Alright," Sebastian said. "Just call me back by tomorrow and let me know."

"Sure." We said our goodbyes and hung up; I dialed Gabby's home number and waited for her to answer.

"Hello?" said a deep, unfamiliar male voice.

"Hey—hello," I said, completely caught off guard.

"Who is this?"

"This is Cara Carson. I'm, uh, calling for Gabby? Gabrielle Moore?" I stuttered.

"Who're you?"

"I'm Gabby's big sister," I said awkwardly.

"Gabby doesn't have a big sister."

Understanding broke over me in a bizarrely dual sensation, first cold, in my hands and feet, and then heat, spreading throughout my body and burning my cheeks.

"You're Gabby's father."

"Is there a problem?"

"What are you doing over there?" I demanded.

"This is my house. Who are you? Gabrielle does *not* have a big sister. Who are you really?"

I hung up. I didn't even know what I was doing. In less time than it should have taken, I was at her house. A shiny blue car was parked in my usual spot in the driveway, so I pulled up to a rough halt across the street, then rushed up the front walk, giving two short courtesy knocks before opening the door. The air inside felt thick and charged.

"Gabrielle!" I called. "It's me. It's Cara."

"What on earth—?" I recognized the man's voice from the phone call. "Did you just let yourself into my house?"

"Cara's here!" I heard Gabby say. She sounded both excited and apprehensive. "Daddy, you can meet Cara."

I stalked into the den to find Mrs. Moore sitting up, head in her hands, crying softly. The television was off. Logan was at his mother's feet, arms wrapped around her ankles, pulling, saying *Momma, Momma,* over and over again. A man was standing in the middle of the room, tall and lean, a pale redhead with narrow shoulders and knobby elbows. I saw where Gabby got her freckles from. I looked from him to Mrs. Moore to Gabby and Logan, marveling at how gorgeous this mixed family was, more whole in their differences than my broken family had ever been. I was caught between a bizarre mix of emotions, from concern for Gabby to a strange anger at her father to something almost like envy, although that seemed like the wrong feeling for the situation.

Gabby was hovering uncertainly between her crying mother and her towering father, looking at Mrs. Moore with concern and Mr. Moore with both admiration and confusion.

"Who are you? What are you doing here?" Mr. Moore demanded.

"I'm being a good big sister to Gabby," I said, unaware that that's what I was going to say, trembling slightly, trying not to let it show. Now that I was here, standing in the middle of everything, I realized how stupid this pseudo-nobility was. My reasonable side suddenly caught up with whatever insanity had possessed me, about ten minutes too late. What the hell was I actually doing?

"I told you this was a bad idea," Mrs. Moore said to her husband. "I told you we should talk without the kids around. This is *not* the time or place." She turned to me and pointed to Gabby. "Take her out of here."

"She will do no such thing," said Mr. Moore, whirling to face me. "I don't know who she is. I don't know what she's doing with my daughter."

"You *left* her—" I started, then clamped a hand over my mouth, which apparently was no longer connected to my brain.

"Cara's a good girl," Mrs. Moore interrupted. "She's been taking good care of Gabby."

I reached out my hand, but Gabby didn't come to me like she normally did. She clung to her father's pants leg and looked at me with wide eyes.

"This is my daddy," she said slowly, as if that explained the entire situation.

"I know. It was nice to finally meet him. But let's go get some dinner, just you and me," I said. "Your parents... have... a lot to talk about."

Gabby let go of her father's leg but stayed put. I took a step forward and grabbed her hand.

"Let me take Logan, too," I said, but it was more of a question directed at Mrs. Moore. She nodded. Without letting go of Gabby's hand, I managed to scoop up Logan and balance him heavily on my hip. He started bawling and twisting to get free.

"What is *going on* here?" bellowed Mr. Moore. "You called *me*, Shauna. You asked me if we could talk. Why is some stranger able to just walk into *my* house and take *my* children?"

"Let them go, Colin," said Mrs. Moore with a sudden steely edge to her voice. Logan was screaming for his mother, throwing the full of his weight away from me.

"We're just going to get dinner, Logan," Gabby said to him, but she sounded uncertain. "Daddy, will you be here when we get back?"

Mr. Moore stood with his hands balled into fists on his waist, glaring at me with an intense stare, but then, as if someone had let the air out of him, he deflated. He hung his head and then knelt down, kissing Gabby's cheek. I tensed as he came closer to me, but he simply leaned in and kissed Logan's forehead. With the squirming Logan trying to break free of my grasp, I turned us all around and marched the kids out of the house. The Moores remained silent behind us as I closed the door and finally exhaled.

Nervous sweat slid down my neck. I got Gabby situated in the back seat, but I didn't know what to do with Logan. I held him on my lap in the front seat, but he flung himself at the car door and beat his pudgy fists against the window, screaming for his mother. I felt like a kidnapper and prayed that there weren't any neighbors watching the scene. Gabby climbed up into the front and tried to comfort him.

"Here, Gabby," I said. "See if he'll calm down for you." I managed to pass him over the center console and place him in the front passenger seat with his sister, where she hugged him tightly and talked to him in a low, soothing voice, a practiced and sisterly tone. With no other ideas, I called my mother.

"Hello?" Mom answered. "Cara, where are you?"

"Mom, I don't know what to do," I said. "Gabby's father showed up, after he left them, after he left the family, and he doesn't deserve to be around the kids, it's not—"

"What?" Mom said, trying to catch up. "Cara, do you think he's violent? Do I need to call the police?"

"No, I don't think he would do anything. He's just mad. But he doesn't deserve to be with his kids now. He left them."

Mom was quiet for a moment on the other end. "What do you need from me?"

"I need... a car seat," I decided. "Or for you to take Logan. But you would still need a car seat."

"Who's Logan?"

"Gabby's little brother. He's about three, I think. Maybe a little younger? I'm pretty sure I need some sort of seat."

"Okay, give me the address. I'll see if I can borrow a car seat from my coworker, and then I'll be on my way."

Between the two of us, Mom and I managed to get Logan strapped securely, if unhappily, into a borrowed car seat. Mom followed me with Logan in her car to a small diner just a couple of blocks from the Moores' house, a busy street cutting their quiet subdivision in half. Undeterred by the evening's events, Gabby chewed happily on onion rings while I played with the straw in my Coke, and Mom broke French fries in half for Logan.

"Thanks for coming, Mom," I said.

"Anything for you, Cara," she said. "But sweetie, I've got to ask, what *happened?*"

I made sure that Gabby was occupied with her food before lowering my voice and leaning forward. "Remember how I told you what happened with Mrs. Moore's baby?"

Mom nodded, still absent-mindedly handing bits of fries to Logan, who hadn't noticed the absence of his mother in the presence of potatoes.

"Mr. Moore left the family because of that, I think. He left either because of the baby or because of how depressed Mrs. Moore's been. I don't know if he's been back at all in the past year, but he was there tonight. He doesn't deserve to just crawl back to his family if he leaves because he can't deal with a tough problem."

Mom pursed her lips, then looked at me for a long moment. I had never really noticed the small lines around her eyes or the streak of grey near her temples, silver strands framing her face.

"May I say something, Cara?"

"Okay," I said, suddenly nervous.

Mom pointed to a glass case of desserts. "Gabby, would you like to go pick out a dessert?"

"Yes!" she squealed, running to it and pushing her nose against the glass. Mom took a deep breath.

"Cara, everyone deals with their problems in different ways. Were Mr. Moore's actions right? Who's to say? All I know is that if I told you that because you pulled away emotionally after Aaron's death that you couldn't come back now, *three* years later, then I would be a miserable woman and a childless mother."

I stared at her, mouth agape.

"I don't think anyone wants to hear harshness or severity from their mother, or from anyone," Mom continued. "But I love you, boundlessly. Endlessly. You know that. And I know I can say this to you because of how far you've come. I'm so happy you're starting to come back to me, Cara. You are my heart. But you, of all people, should understand what it's like to feel that doing your best isn't enough. You know how hard it can be to come back from a tragedy. We're not here to condemn, only to help. And I hope that you can see beyond Mr. Moore's errors, because really, who are we to judge?"

I wanted to cry. But my eyes were wide, dry deserts; I stared shamefully at my hands and waited for Mom to finish.

"I love you, Cara."

And that was it. I realized she was waiting for me to say something back. What could I possibly respond? I settled for the truth.

"I love you, too."

"Bursting into their house and yanking the kids out in a rush was probably overwhelming for Mr. Moore," Mom continued with a little smile. "We don't know anything about their situation. Maybe he left over something different. Maybe they agreed to a year apart. I know you meant well. Actually, seeing you stepping up like that reminded me a lot of Aaron. It's something he would have done, I think. He always charged forward with the best intentions, but sometimes we all need to stop and think and communicate. You could have offered to stay with the kids in their rooms or asked permission to take them."

"I didn't yank them," I said crossly. "And Mrs. Moore did give me permission."

"I just want you to know that in the midst of all of this, how tremendously proud I am of you," Mom said. "Just for doing something. So what do you think would be best to do now?"

"I don't know anymore," I confessed, trying to keep my

voice steady. Exhaustion had crept over me, stealing the place of the adrenaline that had been consuming me and keeping me going.

"I'll come inside when we bring them back," said Mom. "We'll figure something out."

Back at the Moores' household, I was pleased to have Mom at my side, but my heart sank when I realized that the blue car was no longer in the driveway. Gabby peered up and down the street, craning her neck, searching for it.

We went inside to find all of the lights switched on. I gave up trying to hold Logan and set him free in the hallway.

"Mrs. Moore?" I called, peering into the empty living room. Sounds came from the bedroom at the back of the house, and Mrs. Moore walked down the hall towards us, alone. Logan ran to her leg and lifted his arms.

"Momma, where's Daddy?" Gabby asked. Mrs. Moore picked up her son and eyed my mother without saying anything.

"Mrs. Moore? I'm May. I'm Cara's mother," Mom said gently.

"I'm Shauna." She extended a hand to my mother, keeping Logan balanced with her other arm.

"Your daughter is such a joy to be around," Mom said. "And your son is precious. You have beautiful children."

"Thank you."

"I'd like to talk to you, if you have a minute and don't mind," Mom said, offering a friendly smile. Mrs. Moore looked vaguely defeated.

"Alright, then," she answered, sitting down on the sofa,

Logan in her lap. She gestured to Mom to sit beside her. Mom perched on the opposite end of the sofa and placed a hand on the cushion between herself and Mrs. Moore. She drew breath, and I knew she was about to recite the lines that she learned to repeat in so many situations.

"My son passed away three years ago in a car accident. He was coming home from a homecoming party—ironic, isn't it?" She gave her sad, rehearsed little chuckle. She had told this story too many times. I didn't like listening to it, but I wanted to hear what else she had to say.

Mrs. Moore interrupted her. "I assume Cara has told you about our family situation."

"She did."

"Did she also tell you about the various therapists I've been seeing and the different medications I've been taking to try and find something that works? Or did she see me on a couple of bad days and assume I've been neglecting my kids and worse?"

Mom turned to give me a pointed look. I thought I had already reached my peak level of embarrassment in this house. I was wrong.

"Why don't you two go play in another room?" Mom suggested.

"Let's go to Logan's room," I said quickly, leading Gabby out of the den and thinking we might be able to still hear them from there.

"He has boy toys," Gabby said, crinkling her little nose.

"I'd like to see them," I insisted. We went into his room, leaving the door wide open. Gabby opened a toy box by a window and pulled out several small cars. I kept my eyes on the toys but my ears and attention on the sound of the women's voices.

"I'm grateful for Cara, I really am," Mrs. Moore was telling my mother. "Gabby can't stop talking about her. I just want her and Logan to have their mother back, but some days still seem unbearable. I'm trying so hard. I just can't seem to get there."

"It's the hardest thing you'll ever do," Mom said. "I really and truly understand your pain."

"Thank you," said Mrs. Moore. Her voice was thick with tears. "I just can't believe... nine months and then... she was so perfect. They call it being born asleep. I still can't believe it. We were so ready for her. We were so ready."

I moved to the doorway of Logan's room and leaned on the doorframe, waiting for my mother to respond.

"I'm so sorry, Shauna," she said. I waited for her to say that she understood, that she knew how it felt, but she didn't.

"Watch this!" Gabby said, tapping me on the shoulder and racing one of the cars through the air around the room. I followed her half-heartedly with a car of my own, straining to hear what else they were saying.

"After... after it happened... we came back home, and tried to start life over like nothing was wrong. I just couldn't. I told Colin that I needed some space," Mrs. Moore said. "It was a mistake. He's been calling me for the last few months, trying to come back. But with the anniversary of her due date... and the anniversary of when..."

Mrs. Moore drew a deep breath. I had stopped following Gabby around Logan's room, standing still, listening hard.

"It's only been a year," Mrs. Moore continued. "The anniversary was so painful. And Colin just wants... but he can't just expect me to... I'm not ready..."

"Here's the thing," Mom said, and her voice broke. "You will never be ready. You will never be ready to face life without one of your children. You just have to keep moving forward and hope and pray and learn along the way, and before you know it, you'll be so far along, you won't even remember that at one point, you weren't ready. You won't even realize that you still aren't ready."

The two mothers cried softly together, sharing their sorrow, while their daughters played make believe in the next room. I wrenched my attention away and focused instead on Gabby. This was not my conversation to share in. I couldn't fix Mrs. Moore any more than Gabby could fix me. We just had to keep each other company while we walked.

CHAPTER 11

The sharp, shrill ringing of my phone jerked me awake one morning, about two weeks after my fiasco at the Moore house. I had taken Gabby to the planetarium last weekend as planned, and we were supposed to go to the science museum with the Summer Siblings later today. I rolled over in bed, pulled my phone off its charger, and saw *Gabrielle* on the screen. Groggily, I answered.

"Good morning," said someone who was definitely not Gabby. "This is Mrs. Moore."

"Oh," I said, passing my free hand over my eyes and clearing away some of the sleep. I tried to sound more awake. "Good morning."

"Did I wake you up?"

"S'alright," I mumbled. My fuzzy brain struggled to come up with a reason for Mrs. Moore to call me. "Is Gabby okay?"

"She's fine," Mrs. Moore said. "She's been telling me about this museum trip you had planned, but she's not going to be able to go with you today."

"Oh," I said. Then, "Why?"

"I'm taking Gabby and Logan shopping for shoes."

"Oh," I said again.

"Yeah, Gabby's feet have been ready to bust through, and Logan just needs some shoes that can handle how rough he gets," Mrs. Moore continued conversationally.

"Yeah, um, that's probably good," I said, knowing I wasn't making sense.

"I can let you know when we're back, but we might go for lunch or something when we've finished shopping."

"Uh… it might be too late for the museum. It's with the camp. The Summer Siblings," I said stiffly. "I don't pick the times."

"Oh, well. Next time, then," said Mrs. Moore.

"Yeah, sure," I said. "Mrs. Moore…"

"Yes?"

I wanted to ask why she had to pick today, right now, when she knew Gabby already had plans, but I couldn't think of a good way to phrase it without sounding imprudent or rude. The last thing I wanted to do was to put my foot in my mouth again. But she seemed to guess what was on my mind.

"Cara, I have to do this now," she said gently. "I have to. I can't waste any more time. Do you understand?"

"I do," I said, despite feeling miserable. I really did understand.

"Well, you have a good day. Bye," she said, and hung up. I tossed my phone down the length of my bed, where it bounced off the end and clattered to the floor. I tried convincing myself that this was what Gabby and Logan deserved, time with their mother, who loved them dearly. But I, too, loved Gabby dearly, and I didn't know what to do with her being taken away from me.

Don't be dramatic, I reprimanded myself. *She's not being taken away from you. She doesn't belong to you.*

But why had Gabby not been placed in the Summer Siblings camp before this year? I knew the answer: because she wasn't an underprivileged child. Her family wasn't significantly poor, nor did she come from a bad or broken background. It had only been when Mrs. Moore had lost the baby and Mr. Moore had left that she had fallen to the wayside in her own family. And now that Mrs. Moore was even more determined to reclaim her life, Gabby would go back to the stable household she had previously enjoyed. She wouldn't need me anymore.

I shoved my head under my pillow and bit at my lips and my fingers and the sheets until my jaw was exhausted, until I could only focus on the dull ache in my mouth. I was being ridiculous. I was being selfish. I was over-thinking and sliding into delusions and what-ifs, out of the present.

But what if they do take her away from you? whispered that diabolic, relentless little voice. *What if they decide that she no longer meets any requirements for the Summer Siblings and doesn't need a big sister anymore? She's got a real mother and a real brother and certainly doesn't need a fake sister that didn't even really want her in the first place.*

"Shut up," I said out loud, forcing the words out around the mouthful of blanket. There was no going back to sleep at this point. I rolled out of bed and looked at myself blearily in the mirror. A sleep-swollen face, tousled hair, and drawn-down mouth stared back. This was not the face of a competent sibling. This was a face I knew well: the face that follows a loss.

With my day suddenly cleared, I wasn't sure what to do with myself. I picked up my green journal, but I hadn't written in it for a while, and I didn't have anything to say now. I loafed around on the sofa for a bit, but it made me feel uneasy and restless. My sweatpants and oversized t-shirt that I used for pajamas made me feel grimy, like I hadn't showered. I wound up changing into more presentable clothing, but the house still seemed to be closing in around me. A vague sense of hunger only magnified my annoyance.

"Mom, I'm going out," I said finally.

"With Gabby?" she called from the living room.

"Just the opposite," I grumped. "Her mom is taking her shopping, so I'm on my own today."

"That's great news!" Mom exclaimed. "Gabby must be thrilled. I'm so glad!"

"Uh huh," I grunted. Moodily, I slammed the door on the way out, then reopened it and closed it quietly in penance.

I drove around the suburbs for a little bit, twisting through strip mall parking lots and taking speed bumps a little too fast, delighting in bottoming out the car. Eventually, the growling in my stomach grew too loud to ignore, so I made my way to the little coffee shop where our first Summer Siblings meeting had been held.

At the café, I ordered lunch at the counter (no coffee) and tucked myself away in a booth in the back corner. I wished that I had had the foresight to bring a book with me, but I was empty-handed except for my keys, Aaron's keychain, and phone. I stared at a piece of abstract art on the wall, a muddle of reds and golds that did nothing to inspire me, until my food arrived. The chicken salad sandwich somehow managed to look sad. I could only imagine how pitiful I looked, coffee-less at a coffee shop, eating alone.

"Cara?"

I looked up, startled, the sandwich halfway to my mouth. "Chase?"

He was holding a paper cup of coffee and looking down at me and my meal. I felt somewhat trapped in the booth. His hair looked particularly thick and touchable today. I tried not to think about it.

"How are you?" he asked.

"Good, I'm good," I blurted. "How are you?"

"I'm good."

He continued to stand at the side of my table, looking down at me blankly, a bug under a microscope that he didn't really care about. I gestured to the seat across from me. "Do you want to sit, or something...?"

Chase nodded and slid into the seat opposite me. I snuck in a bite of my sandwich as he sat down. Definitely not worth its price. He put his coffee cup down and drummed out a couple of beats with his fingers against the tabletop. I stared into the depths of my tomato slice.

"So, um, I see you're not at the science museum," I said, trying to sound nonchalant.

"Nope," he answered. "Derek is sick. Wish his parents had called and told me before I drove all the way to his house. Figured I'd stop and get some coffee before I went home. I live pretty close to here."

"Oh." I waited for him to ask me why I wasn't at the science museum either, but he just sipped his coffee. I took another bite of sandwich, wondering if I was an awkward chewer. I certainly felt so.

"How's your summer going?" I managed to ask after a

minute. He shrugged a shoulder.

"Not too bad," he said casually. "Not awesome, though. I'm just kind of chilling out."

"No summer job?"

"Nah."

"How come?" I asked, though I wasn't one to talk. Chase blew on his coffee and took a long sip before answering.

"Just didn't want to work," he said finally. "I don't need money. I'm not interested in anything in particular. Like, I'm not dying to be a cashier, you know? I don't like working."

"This Summer Siblings thing is sort of like a job," I commented.

"Uh, I guess so," Chase said, though he didn't sound too sure. "I still have to write that stupid final letter."

"The what?" I asked, curious. No one had mentioned a final letter to me.

"Mrs. Jameson does this thing with letters from the older to younger kids," Chase explained. "You're really not obligated to keep in touch with your kid after you graduate. I mean, some of the crazy ones, like Isa, totally will. But you don't have to. So Mrs. Jameson makes graduated seniors write final letters to their kids after your last summer so they have something to remember you by. It has to be two pages, and full of advice and crap. She makes you do it if you want to list the Summer Siblings on your resume or have her as a reference or something for a job."

"That's actually kind of a nice idea," I mused, picking at my sandwich crust. I had often invented daydreams in which Aaron had left me a last letter, words of wisdom, carrying me through the difficult times in high school like he had always promised. I had even secretly hoped I would find something written to me while we were cleaning out his room. But of course, my imaginative letters were just that—delicious fantasies for my starving mind.

"I guess," Chase said. "I haven't done it yet. But I don't really need this on my resume or anything. I dunno. I might not do it."

"Don't you want Derek to have something from you?"

Chase shrugged without answering.

"How did you... why did you get involved with the Summer Siblings?" I asked, hoping that my question didn't come off offensively.

"I started as a freshman, when I assumed I'd be going to college," Chase said, smirking. "Figured I'd need a club or something to put on transcripts. Never had the heart to just leave Derek in the middle of it, you know? Even by the time I knew for sure I wasn't going to college. Just kind of got stuck."

I wondered, not for the first time, if he would offer an explanation for why he wasn't going to college. He fiddled with the cardboard sleeve on his coffee cup, and I poked at the limp lettuce on my plate, trying to pretend the silence wasn't growing so obviously between us.

"I like having a little sister a lot more than I thought I would," I said into the mounting awkwardness. Chase flicked his hair out of his eyes and nodded a little, but didn't add to the dialogue.

"She's great, Gabby," I chattered on. "She's just so bubbly. Even when she's sad, it's like she knows how to turn it around into happiness. She doesn't let anything negative stick to her." I realized how quickly I was speaking and forced myself to slow down. "She's... helped me a lot more than I think I've helped her, actually."

"I guess I know what you mean," Chase said. He was lean and lanky in the booth seat, slouching a little over his coffee. "Derek is one cool kid. I mean, who knew kids could be, like, funny and smart?"

I wasn't sure what kind of an answer he wanted for that, so I decided to just change the subject. "So, what are your plans after summer ends?"

Chase threw the question back at me. "What are yours?"

I stared at my plate. "I don't really know. I haven't thought much beyond summer."

"Me either."

"I'm trying to, though," I said slowly, for the first time out loud. Tiny, buzzing, nagging thoughts had been plaguing me during the quiet hours before I fully fell asleep and before I fully awoke. The façade of complacency behind which I had been hiding wasn't sitting well with me anymore, not that it ever truly had. It was no longer enough for me to reject the idea of doing anything simply because it didn't matter. I wasn't entirely sure that anything mattered, but I did know that I had to do something, anything, for the sake of simply living. "I'm trying to think of something to do. In life."

"Mm."

I tried again. "What do you do with the time you're not spending with Derek?"

"Uh, I mostly mess around with video games or watch stuff online. Sometimes I just drive around town or hang out." He shifted in his seat. "What about you?"

I thought about it for a minute. "Honestly, I spend a *lot* of time with Gabby, even outside of the Summer Siblings. I read a lot. And, um, I've been dealing with a lot of personal things. Getting through some stuff."

I could tell from the look in his eyes that he was trying to think of Aaron's name, trying to make some sort of connection between me and what had happened. I lifted my chin and forced down the tight feeling in my chest, waiting for Chase to take the conversation away from myself.

"Well, I'm glad I ran into you here," he said after a pause that was just turning stale. "I actually think you're kind of cool." He ducked his head at that, his black hair flopping.

My heart pounded in my chest in a way with which I was not thoroughly familiar. It was not my usual anxiety. Trying to keep my voice light, I mumbled, "Oh, yeah?"

"Yeah. I mean, you're not going to college, you're not working, and you just don't seem to give a damn." Chase looked up at me and gave me a fuller smile than his usual one. My face felt hot. "Most girls are so uptight. You're so laid back about everything. It's cool."

I felt like he was trying to pay me a compliment, but hearing myself described like that dropped something into my stomach quite different from whatever had dropped there at the first sight of Chase. A sensation very similar to guilt slid through me.

"I'm trying, though," I said, confused and honest. "I'm trying to care. I'm trying to give a damn."

"About what?" he asked, just as confused.

I stared at him. I didn't know. I hadn't even been aware that I had been actively trying to care until our conversation.

When I didn't answer, he drummed his fingers once more against the table, then sat up straighter. "Well, I've got to go. Thanks for letting me sit with you. Glad we got to hang out."

"Yeah," I said blankly. "No problem."

"I'll see you around." He slid out of the booth and looked down at me.

"Bye." He lingered by the table for half a moment more, then raised a hand in a silent farewell before sauntering off and leaving the café. The door's little bell jingled as he passed through. I picked at my unfinished sandwich for a while, not eating any more of it, until it was well shredded and smushed, a little fortress with a pickle battalion wall, my straw stuck into it as a pennant. I hoped the waitress would smile at it when she came by to clear the plate. Just in case she didn't, I left a pretty nice tip.

As I sat in my car in the parking lot of the coffee shop, trying to decide what I wanted to do next, my phone buzzed in my pocket.

Pls come home some1 is here 2 c u :-@

Classic Mom text— shortened words and an emoticon that had nothing to do with the actual content. I wondered if Dad had shown up— perhaps I had forgotten another scheduled dinner—or if Mrs. Moore had maybe dropped Gabby off at the house. Brightening at that idea, I headed home.

When I pulled into my own driveway, though, there was a small, dark purple car parked in our driveway. I didn't recognize it at all. Anxiety crept over my shoulders as I hurried into the house through the back door. Mom was brewing coffee in the kitchen.

"Mom, who's here?" I asked quickly, throwing my keys onto the table.

Mom nodded towards the living room. "Earla Jameson. She says she's the director of the Summer Siblings. I don't ever remember meeting her at any conferences or anything at Greenwood. Did you ever have her as a teacher? Does she teach?"

"Oh, God," I said aloud. This was it. She was here to tell me that Gabby didn't need me as a sibling anymore. She would tell me that Gabby had been pulled from camp and that I was out of luck. "Mom, I don't want to talk to her. She's going to take Gabby away."

"Now, why would she do that?" Mom asked me. "You've been such a good big sister to her."

"This is all your fault," I hissed. "You made Mrs. Moore feel better, and now Gabby doesn't meet camp qualifications anymore. They're going to pull her out of the program. That's what Mrs. Jameson's here to tell me."

"Cara, that's—that's a ridiculous idea," Mom spluttered. The coffee maker gurgled by her elbow. Turning from me, she pulled out two mugs. "All I did was share my story with Shauna. Now you take this cup—" she poured hot coffee into one of them— "to Mrs. Jameson, and I'll join you in just a minute. Go on, now."

I stood for a second, glaring at her and the coffee mug, before taking it and walking unsteadily into the living room. Mrs. Jameson was sitting comfortably in our recliner. She pulled her glasses down a bit and smiled at me over the frames as I handed her the coffee.

"Hello, Cara, dear," she said warmly. I gave her a quick, tight-lipped smile and sat stiffly across from her on the edge of the sofa. She looked like the subject of a masterful painting, an anachronism in the midst of our outdated living room.

"How are you?" she asked.

"I'm fine," I said curtly. Then, feeling rude, "How are you?"

"I'm doing well," she said. "Your mother has been very kind sitting with me while we waited for you to come home."

"Shouldn't you be at the science museum with the Summer Siblings?"

"That ended about an hour ago. I came straight here afterwards."

"Why were you waiting for me to come home?" I couldn't stop myself from sounding a bit snappy.

"I just wanted to drop by and talk to you about how things are going with Gabby," Mrs. Jameson said, smiling around the mug as she pressed it to her lips.

"They're *fine*," I said emphatically. "Gabby is *great*. She—she loves me."

"I have no doubt that she loves you, dear," said Mrs. Jameson. "In fact, I just spoke with her mother this morning."

"You what?"

"I called Shauna Moore to check in on how everything was going."

"You—but, why?"

Mrs. Jameson saw my expression and chuckled. "Relax, Cara, dear. I always call the families of the children, or the children themselves, about once a month to see how things are going. It's part of my job, you see."

"Oh," I said, a bit stupefied. "Wow. That must be a lot of work."

"I enjoy it," replied Mrs. Jameson. "I get to see the differences you all are making in these children's lives. It's beautiful."

I nodded mutely.

"Well, Shauna and I had a lovely conversation," Mrs. Jameson said, "Would you like to know what she told me?"

"Only if it's good," I said quickly. Mrs. Jameson laughed.

"To be honest, Cara, dear, I wasn't sure if I made the right decision by letting you join after graduation, especially since I was not entirely certain about your, shall we say, intentions. You see, I was worried you would use Gabrielle to help yourself more than you would help her. Really, you have my friend Audie to thank for your position here. But you know that. I digress."

I hung my head, looking at my hands sitting idly in my lap, deeply ashamed. It was one thing to know it within myself, and another to hear someone tell me plainly and have her try to look me in the eye. Mrs. Jameson seemed to be waiting for me to say something, but I couldn't. I compromised by forcing myself to look directly at her.

"But I am happy to concede that I was wrong," Mrs. Jameson continued. "Despite whatever your feelings were when you started, it seems that you have been truly lovely with Gabby. Mrs. Moore thinks very highly of you and had nothing but compliments on the phone. I wanted to come and thank you in person."

"That's it?" I blurted in surprise.

"You have been a wonderful sister to Gabrielle, a very positive influence and role model for her to look up to. You brought fun activities for her to escape in when her family life had collapsed around her. I think knowing her daughter was safe and secure with someone helped put Mrs. Moore's mind at ease so she could better focus on herself. We had a long chat today about her family. Sometimes the smallest things make such a difference." Mrs. Jameson was smiling. "It's rare that I see this kind of change happen over the course of a summer. Most of our children come from poverty or broken homes. Our teenagers can't change the situations, and their goal is usually just to provide some extra fun and love for a lonely child. And that's a beautiful thing, and I'm so proud to help it happen. But I have been exceptionally thrilled with how you and Gabrielle have bonded."

"Mrs. Jameson," I started, the heat in my cheeks making resurgence. "It was very nice of you to come all the way out here just to say that to me. But... I didn't do anything. I said stupid things and made assumptions. My mom was the one who really figured everything out."

"I'm pleased to hear you're able to admit your own mistakes," said Mrs. Jameson. She leaned forward and placed her coffee on our end table, then leaned back and settled into the chair. "But don't forget to look at your successes, too. Mrs. Moore told me you tried to talk to her, and always called for permission to take Gabby out, and that you took care of Gabby and her brother when their father returned. Now, Mrs. Moore was the only one with the power to help herself, but you're playing a part in this. You see, being present for Gabby, small of a thing as it may seem, has made a noticeable difference."

I couldn't believe Mrs. Jameson was complimenting me on actually being present. I should ask her to call up Audie Wells and say it again.

"You make it sound so..." I sighed, trying to think of a good word. "You make me sound brave and good. I'm not."

"What was it you told me before?" Mrs. Jameson asked. "That we help each other heal?"

I blinked.

"I think you're afraid I'm going to accuse you of being healed by Gabby," Mrs. Jameson said. "I was only worried that you would try to find healing without giving anything in return. We are meant to learn from others, Summer Siblings included. Many of our teenagers are reintroduced to the childlike joy their siblings show them. They learn and grow and, yes, some heal. My dear, you and Gabby have given and taken equally, I think. I'm here to encourage that."

"No," I said, ashamed. "She gives so much more."

Mom finally bustled into the living room with her coffee in one hand and a plate of cookies in the other. I recognized them as leftovers from Gabby's sleepover.

"So sorry," Mom apologized. "Would you like a cookie, Earla?"

"I was just about to head out," Mrs. Jameson said. She smiled at my mother, who smiled back, like they were sharing a secret. I suspected Mom had not been so busy with getting the cookies as just waiting in the kitchen for the right moment to walk in. "But I'd be happy to take one for the road."

I got up and followed her to the front door. She paused to readjust her sheer scarf, peering into the mirror hanging on the wall.

"Mrs. Jameson?"

"Yes, dear?"

"Thank you for taking the time to stop by."

"Just part of what I do," she said, smiling broadly. "I trust you've got something planned for what to do from here, for Gabby and for yourself. Summer doesn't last forever."

"I'm working on it," I lied, trying to convince myself that

it was only a partial lie. I *wanted* to think of something, to have a plan. I just *couldn't*. "I actually just learned today about the final letter that you have seniors write. But I'd like to keep in touch with Gabby beyond that. I'm just not sure what I'll actually be doing after summer ends. I'm really thinking about it, though."

"I'm sure you are," said Mrs. Jameson. "I have enormous faith in you, Cara, dear." She looked as if she wanted to hug me, but pulled open the door instead and walked into the sunlight outside. I squinted at her retreating figure until she got into her car, gave me a wave, and drove off. I desperately wished she would take some of that faith back.

Mom came to stand by me in the doorway as I stared out into the empty street. "I'm so proud of you, sweetie."

Her pride and affirmation dug into my side just as sharply as Mrs. Jameson's had. "I'm not really all that great, Mom. Everything you guys think I did wasn't that incredible."

Mom pulled me towards her and kissed me on top of my head. She was a few inches taller than me, even with her shoes off.

"Everything you do is incredible. Everything you are is incredible," she said into my hair.

"Stop it, Mom. You have to say that."

"I believe it with every fiber in my being," she said gently. She gave my shoulders a squeeze and a final kiss atop my head. "I believe in you."

I mimed gagging at the cheesiness, but I hugged her back. The intangible faith and belief resting on my shoulders were nearly more than I could bear, a heavy weight and physical burden. I tried to straighten my back, as if I were balancing a book on my head, neck held high like a ballerina, but the new posture was uncomfortable. But I recognized a change in me: whereas before, I would have immediately shrugged it off, I now hoped to grow used to it. I wanted to learn how to carry it.

CHAPTER 12

July blazed on, sweltering and steaming. Over the past month, Gabby and I had made ourselves regulars at Pop's Ice Cream Parlor. The employees all recognized us and knew Gabby by name, often offering a free topping for her ice cream. I was wondering if Mrs. Moore might let me take Gabby for ice cream again, or if she would be too busy assimilating back into normal life, when Sebastian called.

"Aquarium trip tomorrow," he reminded me. "Should be one of our best outings. Lots of fun and free air conditioning."

I chuckled. "Gabby's been looking forward to this one ever since I told her about it at the beginning of summer."

"So we'll see you there?"

"I have to check," I sighed.

"Okay, call me back by tonight."

"Sebastian? Can I ask you something?"

"Sure."

"Will Ms. Wells... I mean, will Audie be there tomorrow?"

"Yep. Why?"

"No reason," I said casually, though I had been thinking that maybe it was time I stopped avoiding her. Sebastian hung up, and I was now faced with calling Mrs. Moore to ask for permission.

But I had worried for nothing. "Sure thing, Cara," she said when I called. I could hear Gabby cheering in the background.

"You have fish on your shirt!" she said gleefully when I came to pick her up. I had dug through the depths of my closet until I found it—a light blue shirt with a massive orange fish and a bright yellow starfish, with the words "Fish Upon a Star" written in bubbly letters. It was an old shirt, some distant relative's idea of a great gift, and kind of stupid, but for the purposes of today and seeing Gabby smile, it was worth it.

"Have you ever been to the aquarium, Gabby?" I asked.

"We were supposed to go for a field trip last year," she said, "but I was sick and had to stay home."

"Well, I guess it's your lucky day!" I said. She beamed from the back seat.

I paid the fee to park in front of the aquarium in a lot that was designed to look underwater. Enormous abstract murals of fish and exotic sea animals gazed down at us from the tall building walls. Gabby clung to my hand and stared back up at the paintings with wide eyes.

I could see our group waiting just outside of the entrance. Adam and Evan were playing with their ever-present hacky sack, kicking it between the two of them. I recognized Nicole and her little sister, Louise, from the park, and a couple others whose names I had tried to memorize over the course of the summer. Isa showed her teeth in something like a smile as we approached. She was holding Nina's hand and had her other hand on the shoulder of Kimmy, Julie's little sister.

"Hi, Gabrielle," she said cheerfully. Then, less upbeat, "Hi, Cara. You and Gabrielle need to go see your counselor so he can stamp your hand. That proves you're part of our group and that your ticket came through us."

"Where's Julie?" I asked.

"She had to go to early orientation for her university today," Isa said. "But she didn't want Kimmy to miss out on any fun, and neither did I! She asked me if I could help out, so I picked Kimmy up for her, so we can all have fun together." She patted Kimmy's shoulder, who smiled up at her gratefully. I had to give her credit—no matter how she acted towards me, she was nothing but sweet towards the kids.

"That's pretty cool," I said, and I meant it. "I'm glad you could still come, Kimmy." I felt guilty at not having thought to do the same for Gabby when we missed the trip to the zoo thanks to my dentist appointment. I made a mental note in the event that I wouldn't be able to make it to any of the remaining camp outings.

Holding Gabby's hand, I turned to find Sebastian amidst the kids, teenagers, and other green-shirted counselors. As luck would have it, he was chatting with Ms. Wells. I took a breath and approached them. They were so engrossed in their conversation that they didn't look up until I was standing right in front of them.

"Cara!" Ms. Wells said, smiling widely at me as I stood there. "How wonderful to see you!"

"I think we're supposed to get our hands stamped," I said to Sebastian.

"Here you go," he said, pressing a rubber stamp to the back of each of our hands.

"It's a starfish!" Gabby giggled. "Just like Cara's shirt!"

"Ms. Wells? Can I speak with you?" I asked.

"Of course," she said. She handed her clipboard, stamp, and ink pad to Sebastian. "Hold onto those for me?"

"Hey, go ask Adam and Evan if they'll let you play with their ball." I nudged Gabby towards the boys. "Look, I see Amber and Kirsten over there, too."

Gabby ran off. Ms. Wells and I walked a little bit away from the larger group. She was wearing sneakers in place of her usual kitten heels; I had never seen her dressed so casually. She clasped her hands together and looked at me expectantly.

"Are we speaking professionally?" she asked. "Or casually?"

Her face remained neutral as I considered her words. Did I want to talk to her as my therapist, or simply as a summer camp counselor whom I happened to know? "Can it be both?"

"Let's try it. What did you want to talk about?"

"I just wanted to say thanks, I guess," I said. "For... suggesting this for me. And for encouraging me."

"You're welcome," she beamed. "I knew you could do it. I knew you could push yourself forward."

"Thanks," I said again. We stood in silence for a minute. "Sorry I've been kind of avoiding you."

"It's alright," she answered. "I probably should have told you that I work with the Summer Siblings. I'm sorry you got blindsided by it. I just didn't want you to say no to the opportunity because of me. I can only imagine how odd it must be to see me outside of... the office."

"Yeah," I said. "Not too weird, though. You're so nice.

Of course you would volunteer for something as great as this."

"You're very kind," she laughed. I smiled back, realizing I hadn't ever heard her truly laugh during our serious sessions. More silence, but the comfortable kind. Unlike our appointments, I didn't feel like I was wasting my mom's money by not talking.

"May I direct this conversation away from professional and towards casual?" she asked.

"Sure."

"He's kind of cute, isn't he?" Ms. Wells pointed subtly at Sebastian.

"Oh, my God," I gasped. I couldn't help but laugh. "Too casual!"

"Sorry," she said, embarrassed but still smiling. "I thought maybe we were getting a little too close to our usual conversations."

"You like him?" I asked. She grinned at me and shrugged. I tried to picture the baby-faced-but-goateed Sebastian with the prim and neat Audie. I laughed again.

"Cara, let's gooo!" Gabby called, running up to us. She tugged on my arm and tried to pull me towards the aquarium doors. "I'm no good at the hacky ball thing. I want to go see the fish!"

"Take a chill pill," I advised her, smiling. "The counselors will let us know when we can go in. I think we're probably still waiting for Mrs. Jameson."

"That's right," Ms. Wells told Gabby. "If you can be patient for just a little longer, it will most definitely be worth it. We'll go in soon."

"I don't wanna be patient," she whined, but then she stood up straight and suddenly held out her hand. "I don't know you. My name is Gabrielle Moore."

"Do you often introduce yourself to strangers?" I chuckled, but Ms. Wells shook Gabby's hand seriously.

"My name is Audie Wells."

"I like your name," Gabby sighed dreamily. "It's so much prettier than Gabrielle!"

"Gabrielle is a beautiful name," Ms. Wells told her.

"Her name is Cara," Gabby said, pointing at me. "She's my big sister." Ms. Wells laughed and shook my hand, too.

"Cara, it is an absolute pleasure to meet you," she said, winking. I dipped my head.

"Hello, all you wonderful Summer Siblings!" rang the cheerful voice of Mrs. Jameson as she walked towards the group. Her ultramarine scarf looked like shimmering water as it flowed behind her in her wake. She was carrying an enormous tote bag and a megaphone. "Can everyone hear me?"

We gathered in a lopsided circle around her as she held the megaphone up to her mouth.

"This is our most attended event yet! I'm so excited to see so many of you here. Because we have so many siblings present, we're going to go through the aquarium in smaller groups. Stay with your counselor and follow their instructions. You'll be free to do a little wandering on your own at the end. Any questions?"

No one raised a hand. The sun beat down on us relentlessly.

"No? Okay. Find your counselor, and remember, have fun!"

"Who's our counselor?" Gabby asked me.

"Sebastian. He just stamped our hands, remember?"

"Oh. I was kind of hoping it would be Ms. Audie," she said, visibly disappointed. "She's nice. And pretty."

"And I hear she has a pretty name," I reminded her. "But we're stuck with Sebastian."

"Aw, I'm sorry about that," Sebastian said, overhearing us. "I promise I'll try to look as pretty as Audie does." He batted his eyes behind his huge glasses at Gabby, who cracked up.

Something soft but solid hurtled into my leg. I reached down and picked up the hacky sack from the ground.

"Did you kick this at me?" I demanded of Adam, who was grinning.

"Sorry," he said. "Those things can be really hard to control."

"Yeah!" Evan giggled.

"Looks like we're in the same group," Adam said. "Isa, too. Our counselor Dawn's not here today, so Mrs. J split up our group."

"How am I supposed to survive both you and Isa?" I asked, only half joking.

"Kimmy's with us!" Gabby squealed as Isa walked Nina and Kimmy over. I tried to pin the names of siblings together as everyone gathered around Sebastian: Amber and Kirsten, Lisa and Shelley, Patrick and Timothy, Hayley and Tara... how much would I have to interact with them? I barely recognized half of our smaller group. I could feel the familiar fog quietly creeping over my mind, separating me from the situation, but Gabby's small hand slid into mine, and she held me there, an anchor in the present.

"Alright, guys!" Sebastian called. Sweat beaded on his forehead. "Let's go inside and see some fish!"

I let Gabby tug me into the aquarium, trailing at the back of our group. Goosebumps erupted down my arms as we walked into the freezing lobby, but the cold was welcome.

"Where are we going first? I want to see dolphins! Do they have octopuses?" Gabby asked excitedly, scampering in a circle around me.

"Octopi," corrected Isa.

"I don't think they have dolphins here, Gabs," I said. "Our aquarium's not that big. But they should have an octopus or two."

"Or eight," giggled Nina. "It's funny because octopi have eight legs. Eight octopi with eight legs would be…"

"A million legs!" shrieked Kimmy. The girls cackled hysterically. I wasn't sure what was funny about it, but I indulged in a chuckle, anyway. I was delighted by how nonsensical these conversations could turn.

"Where to first, Captain?" Adam called ahead to Sebastian. He consulted his clipboard.

"We'll go through the first couple of displays together, and then our group is going to go to the sting ray exhibit. Then we'll head to the sea turtle tanks, then the tropical fish section, and then you'll have about fifteen minutes to wander on your own. Everyone *must* meet up at the café by the gift shop after that. Understand?"

Everyone nodded. I was putting almost my full weight into holding Gabby back and keeping her from running ahead.

"Can we go *now?*" she begged.

"We have to follow Sebastian," I told her. He turned on his heel and led us forward.

Immediately beyond the entrance was an enormous

tunnel that spanned down the length of a hallway. Thick acrylic glass made a parabola of an aquarium over our heads, so that fish swam around us on all sides. A lone shark sliced his way through the water, while a manta ray glided high above, like a bizarre, underwater bird of prey.

"I don't wanna walk through there," Gabby said, stopping abruptly. "I don't like it."

I knelt down beside her. "What's wrong?"

She pointed up at the shark and repeated, "I don't like it. What if it breaks and the shark gets us?"

I wondered how to respond. I wasn't sure if it would be more comforting to lie and say it was impossible, or to give her the straight truth about how in the unlikely event that it did happen, we'd have to worry about being crushed by the falling glass and weight of the water, not a flopping shark. I shook my head. "How about I carry you through? If we see the glass breaking, I'll make a run for it and save you."

Gabby stamped her feet, a high-pitched whine issuing from her mouth. I rarely saw her like this. I reached out to grab her hand, but she flailed her arms away from me and let out a little shriek. Sebastian and the rest of the group had moved beyond the mouth of the tunnel, leaving us alone at the entrance.

"Gabby, if you don't go through this tunnel, we can't go to the rest of the aquarium," I told her sternly, lowering my voice as hers heightened. She continued to make indistinct noises of frustration.

"Okay..." I said, standing and moving away from her slowly. "I guess I'll go through by myself... I can't wait to see all the fish..."

"Wait!" she cried, reaching out to me, her feet still

planted. I came back to her and crouched down, then let her jump up on my back. She wrapped her legs around my waist, and I took off into the tunnel, carrying her piggyback style. Gabby tightened her arms around my neck as she stared in awe at the creatures swimming above us.

"Are you sure they can't get us?" she squeaked. I tried to answer, but she was pressing tightly against my vocal cords, so I nodded my head and plodded through the tunnel until we reached the end, where she slid off my back. She stood still for a moment, then walked, with baby steps, to the edge of the tunnel, peering up at the glass.

"They really, really can't get us?"

"They really can't," I said. She hesitated, then placed her hand flat against the glass. A fish darted away from the movement. Gabby jerked back immediately, spinning around and looking for me, but when she saw I was smiling, she laughed.

"I scared a fish!" she grinned.

"I saw!" I said. "That wasn't too bad, was it?"

The rest of the group hadn't raced through the tunnel as we did; they were taking their time, pointing at all of the sea life surrounding them. Gabby and I practiced taking small steps into the mouth of the tunnel, seeing how far she could get before running back. I couldn't believe the magnitude of pride I felt when she made it to the middle without realizing it. Sebastian eventually signaled for everyone to move on.

The room to which the tunnel led had a wide, open floor plan with colorful, plexiglass fish and seaweed sculptures bursting from the floor. Huge tanks, recessed into the walls, displayed hundreds of different fish. One wall was made up entirely of a tank from floor to ceiling, from which Gabby kept a safe distance. The other three walls had multiple smaller tanks teeming with sea life. From across the room, Gabby pointed at the wall-to-wall tank.

"Look at them all!" she cried. Kimmy ran straight up to the tank, pressing her nose to the glass and pointing out some of the flashier fish with their sleek bodies. Isa joined her and expertly directed her attention to the coral at the bottom of the tank.

"See the moray eel?" she said, pointing at a thick, ugly creature with a shockingly wide eye that seemed to be looking right at me. "Moray eels look scary, but they're really not. They just have bad eyesight, and only bite humans if they can't tell the difference between fingers and food. Most eels like to hide in cracks and crevices, which is where you'll see their heads poking out."

I rolled my eyes. She was reading straight from a plaque that was bolted to a little stand just in front of the tank, but Gabby listened closely, mouth agape.

"Let's check out the little tanks," I suggested. "Look, have you ever seen a lionfish before?" I led her to a smaller tank that contained two spiny creatures. I glanced at the tank's plaque with the scientific name, hoping to glean a fun fact to parrot like Isa. *Pterois.* I couldn't even pronounce it.

"Those don't look like lions," Gabby said, frowning at the tank's occupants.

"You're right. They just look plain *weird*," I joked. Gabby spared the lionfish a moment more before racing to the next tank.

"Seahorses!" she said, her eyes lighting up as she recognized the curly-cue tails. Evan ran up next to her and made a loud whinnying sound in her ear.

"They're not *real* horses, Evan," she told him impatiently. "Just like the lionfish aren't real lions." She looked up at me; I nodded in confirmation.

Just after we had made two full, slow rounds of the room, and Gabby was starting to get antsy, Sebastian led the group down a hallway and to the right. Squinting at his clipboard, I could see elaborately drawn paths in different colors on his map. Mrs. Jameson must have worked hard to make sure everyone got to have fun without being overcrowded.

I gathered my courage and initiated conversation. "Mrs. Jameson really puts her heart into this stuff."

"Heart and soul," Sebastian agreed. "Woman's a saint."

My thoughts floundered, trying to come up with something new to say. "How long have you been working as a counselor with her?"

"This is my third year. I have a degree in social work, and during the school year, I work as a counselor at an elementary school. That's how Mrs. Jameson found me."

"Cool," I said, storing that tidbit of information away. We walked through a set of large double glass doors to see a low tank, more like a wading pool with a barrier, and several attendants— the stingray exhibit.

"Hi, guys! Welcome to our underwater petting zoo. Here, you have the chance to pet our friendly stingrays. I know they have the word *sting* in their name, but I promise that they will not hurt you."

The attendant's speech sounded rehearsed, but at least he wasn't monotoning his way through it. He did, however, look like he'd rather be anywhere else. "We've taken off the parts that sting, which are called the barbs. But we didn't hurt the stingrays… it's just like filing their fingernails."

Gabby dug her own fingernails into the palm of my hand and tried to stifle her laughter when I jumped.

"Okay, everyone look at my hands. Make a peace sign!" The kids obediently held up two fingers in a V. "Now bring those two fingers together. This is how you will pet the stingrays, right on their backs. Don't pet them like you would pet a dog. Just use these two fingers. Who wants to go first?"

Gabby turned and looked at me, as if she needed permission. But even though I nodded encouragingly at her, she didn't step up. Kids started crowding the edge of the tanks.

"Let's do it together," I said, kneeling down so I was at her height. She twisted her arms behind her back and gave me a look. This trip was really bringing out Gabby's fearful side.

"I'm a little freaked out, too," I told her. Come to think of it, I really didn't want to stick my arm into a tank full of stingrays, despite their lack of barbs. "On three?"

Gabby stuck her tongue out just a little bit, but stepped up to the tank. I held out my two fingers, and she mimicked the motion.

"One... two... three!" I said, then plunged my arm into the tank, cold water up to my elbow. Gabby followed just a half-second after. I tried not to squeal as a stingray swam up under my hand, velvety in a wet sort of way. Gabby jerked her hand out as soon as she touched one, her eyes huge.

"I did it!" she yelled. I let one more pass under my hand before pulling my own arm out. Who could have ever guessed that a stingray would feel like a flat, luxurious, underwater cushion? I stared at Gabby, who was dipping her hand back in and out again. I wondered about the other things I might have missed out on in my life because I was too scared. What other marvelous things had I passed by? What other sensations, feelings, tastes, memories had I ignored in my passivity?

"Everyone ready?" Sebastian called, after all the kids who had wanted to pet the stingrays had done so. Another group of Summer Siblings idled behind us, waiting to see the exhibit. I spotted Chase and Derek standing in the back. We followed Sebastian where he led us, gazing at the peaceful sea turtles with their mosaic shells, gasping at the intensity of the coloration of the tropical fish. We passed other exhibits but couldn't stop; Sebastian explained we only had a limited amount of time with our special, discounted group passes. He finally announced that it was time for our fifteen free minutes and made us all individually promise him that we would meet back at the café afterwards.

"So where are you two ladies going from here?" Adam asked me as the group started to split up. Nina and Kimmy were dragging Isa, who looked less than thrilled, back to the stingray exhibit.

"I don't know," I said. "What do you want to see next, Gabs?"

"Dolphins!"

"I still don't think there are any dolphins here," I told her. "But I know they've got lots of other cool stuff."

"Like what?"

"Like jellyfish," Evan piped up. "That's what we're going to see."

"Ewww," Gabby wrinkled her nose. "I hate jellyfish. I wanna see penguins."

"Sounds like we've got ourselves a plan," I said. "To the penguin exhibit!"

"We'll walk with you," Adam said. Gabby bounced around, singing some sort of penguin-themed song, and seemed to have no intention of stopping. Evan pulled at my shorts.

"How come she likes penguins so much?" he asked me.

"I don't think that she actually does," I mused. "She's just easily excitable."

"That's dumb."

"Hey, man," Adam reprimanded him. "Be nice. You love frogs. I've seen your froggy backpack and your frog stuffed animals. Not to mention your frog hat with the eyes on top."

"So what?"

"Sooo," Adam said, "everyone loves something like that. Everyone's got that one thing that they like that might not make sense to others. Yours is frogs. Mine is macaroni and cheese. Man, do I love mac and cheese. Gabby's is penguins."

"It's not," I interjected. "She likes everything. Although pizza and ice cream might be her thing. Well, things, plural."

"What's yours?" Adam asked.

"My what?"

"Your thing. The thing you love to an unhealthy degree that normal people just kind of, you know, like. An obsession, if you will. What's your obsession? What's your frogs? What's your pizza and ice cream?" He pretended to point a microphone at me, an interviewer with the million dollar question. *"What's your mac and cheese?"*

I looked at him. "Nothing."

"Nothing? Seriously? No TV show, or maybe you just really love pen twirling, or breakfast foods, or something? Or maybe you're really awesome at crossword puzzles. Anything?"

In the past three years, I had often experienced the sensation of being looked at as if an x-ray were exposing me, as my parents, Ms. Wells, and teachers tried to search me for whatever I was really thinking. As if they wanted to look into the depths of me, and upon doing so, would find something worth mentioning. For the first time, I felt the opposite— as if the way Adam was looking at me revealed nothing on the inside. I felt empty. Useless.

"Don't you have any hobbies at all?" he asked.

"I mean, I guess I like reading," I said defensively. I thought of how Ms. Wells had recognized in me the ability to write, even though I hadn't touched my journal in a while. "And writing, I guess."

Adam nodded. "Okay. You guess. Anything else?"

"Spending time with Gabby," I said.

"What's your favorite book?"

"I can't pick. I don't have one."

"What's your favorite food?"

"Random," I accused. "And I don't know."

"You know, Cara," Adam said, his tone changing suddenly. "You can't go on like this forever."

"Wow," I said, offended. "You can be a real—" I looked at the two kids walking with us and changed my choice of word. "—jerk."

"And you can be a real pessimist," Adam said, cheerfully. His upbeat attitude made me want to slug him.

"Why do you persist in torturing me?" I demanded.

"It's what friends do," he chuckled, holding open a door for me. Gabby and I walked through to see an enormous wall of glass, behind which swam a dozen penguins.

"Penguins!" Gabby yelled. "I see penguins!"

"If, you know, you even want a friend," Adam said, his voice a little lower. "I'm here for you."

Gabby tugged on my hand.

"You ladies have fun," he added. "Ready to see those jellyfish, Evan?"

"Yeah!"

Gabby stood before the great glass wall, craning her neck up to see the ice at the top where some penguins were waddling. I glared at Adam, confused about the direction our conversation had taken.

"I suggest you get a weird hobby," Adam told me, cracking his usual little grin. "Or an obsession. They can be fun, if not a little terrifying and life-consuming. In the best way possible, of course."

"Thanks for your *suggestions*," I said sharply. "I'll be sure to take them and every precious word you've said into consideration when planning out my life."

"Good to hear you're actually making a plan," Adam said, winking at me, and then walking on with Evan. I stared after him in frustration until Gabby pulled my wrist again and pointed to the penguins.

"They're so funny," she giggled. "They're birds, but they can't fly!"

"Gabby, a word of advice," I said. "Just get a weird hobby or obsession now so you don't have to deal with dumb people later in your life."

"Whatever, Care-uh!" she said, as she always did whenever something I said went over her head.

"I'm just saying," I smiled. "I'm just saying."

CHAPTER 13

Bathed in the turquoise light filtering through the water of the exhibit, Gabby stared starry-eyed at the penguins, her gaze never leaving the graceful arcs and twirls of the birds in the water. She gasped in delight at their underwater acrobatics, running up and down the length of the wall and spinning and leaping as best as she could in imitation.

It really was an impressive display, but I moved restlessly around the exhibit, watching the people watching the penguins. Our fifteen minutes passed too quickly; I hated dragging Gabby away when she was so enthralled.

"Bye, penguins," she said sadly, her little head drooping as we walked away towards the café. I could see Isa already sitting there with Nina and Kimmy. Other Summer Siblings members were grouped around their respective counselors. Sebastian waved us over.

"You'd think that when we say fifteen minutes, people would actually show up after fifteen minutes," he griped. "It'll probably be a full half hour before everyone wanders down here."

"What happens if people just don't show up?" I asked.

"We'll make an announcement over the aquarium's intercom. Can't lose any kids. We wind up having to do this almost everywhere we go. People get wrapped up in their own things."

"Ah," I said, distracted. Adam and Evan were heading our way. I looked in the opposite direction. "Hey, if it's going to take a bit for others to come down, do you think I could take Gabby to the gift shop right there?"

"Huh?" Sebastian looked up from his clipboard, where he was checking off names. "Sure. Just stay close and listen for when we're leaving."

"Great, thanks," I said, hurrying Gabby towards the gift shop. I didn't feel like being caught in a triangle of Isa bossiness and Adam irritation. "Let's go look at the souvenirs, Gabs."

"Ooooh!" Gabby squealed. The gift shop was only a little way down from the café, but it was far enough. I could still see the lime green shirts of the counselors if I poked my head out into the corridor. We were surrounded by an enormous assortment of souvenirs that seemed vaguely grouped around a nautical theme. I saw everything from fish-shaped plates to toy boats to anchor earrings. Anything that could be sold.

We wandered between rows of over-priced stuffed animals and key chains, Gabby touching everything she could. She picked up a plush stingray and swam it up and down an aisle, while I looked at some shirts with fish motifs.

"None of those shirts are as good as yours," Gabby said disapprovingly. She handed me the stingray. It felt velvety, exactly like the live ones. I checked the price tag—a little steep, but I had enough.

"Do you want this stingray, Gabby?"

"You mean I could have something?" she asked, her face glowing. "We could buy something?"

"Sure. You can pick one thing, within reason," I added, sounding like my mom. Spinning spastically in a circle, the whirling dervish I took to be Gabby poked and prodded every item the shelves had to offer. I stepped out for a second to check on the Summer Sibilngs. Still there.

"This is what I want," Gabby said, holding something behind her back.

"That's it?" I asked, reaching behind and taking it from her. It was a small plastic starfish attached to a long cord, a pendant that would hang down to her bellybutton if she wore it. "Are you sure?"

"It's a necklace," she informed me, grabbing it back.

"You're sure you don't want a stingray? Or a penguin?" I asked, indicating the large wall of stuffed animals behind us.

"It looks like the starfish on your shirt," she explained, pointing. "I wanna be like you, Cara!"

I looked down at the little girl, who beamed back up at me, holding the star. I thought of Aaron's penny keychain with the stamped out star shape. With a start, I realized I had left it at home today. My heart swelled.

I paid for the necklace at the register, then turned to Gabby. "Want to wear this right now?"

"Yes, yes, yes!"

I hung it around her neck, holding onto the star for a second longer.

"Now we match," Gabby said. "We're fishalicious!"

"How do you even come up with stuff like that?" I asked

her, laughing. She shrugged and giggled.

"Would all members of the Summer Siblings please report to the café? Your group is waiting for you. All Summer Siblings members, please report to the café." The voice echoed through the gift shop, streaming from the intercoms. I glanced back at the café, where Sebastian looked up and caught my eye, waving me back over.

"Okay, time to go back to the group," I said to Gabby. "Actually, you know what? You go ahead and tell Sebastian I'll be down in a minute."

"Why?"

"Because I asked you to."

"Why?"

I sighed. "Because it's a surprise."

"Okay!" Gabby said, dancing out of the gift shop, her plastic star bouncing against her small frame. Quickly, I turned and grabbed a little stuffed penguin from the shelf, just bigger than my hand, and took it to the cash register. I thought it would be a nice surprise for Gabby when I dropped her off back home. Or maybe I could give it to her at the end of the summer, when she returned to school. Maybe I could put it with my final letter to her. I handed the cashier my debit card, checking over my shoulder all the while to make sure Gabby didn't creep up behind me and see her surprise.

I walked back to the Summer Siblings group, the gift bag stuffed into my purse. Sebastian looked up at me.

"There you are. You're the last of my group," he said as I approached. "You're free to go now."

"Where's Gabby?" I asked.

"With you," Sebastian said slowly.

"No," I said, my heart doing a peculiar twist inside my

chest. "I sent her from the gift shop to tell you I was coming. It was only a minute ago. Sixty seconds. Not even that long."

"Maybe she stayed in the gift shop," Sebastian suggested.

"No, I just came from there," I said, my voice rising.

"Stay calm. We have kids wander off every so often. I'll go check the gift shop. You check around the café," Sebastian told me, taking on an air of authority. He took off. I felt like I was wearing lead boots.

"Gabby?" I called, trying to keep my voice steady. I checked behind a large cardboard cutout of a cartoon whale. Nothing. My heart quickened. "Gabrielle!"

Still nothing. I ran out to the open space between the gift shop and the café, desperately scanning the faces of the people milling around me, not registering anything, desperate to recognize Gabby's freckled face. "GABRIELLE!"

"What's wrong?" Adam asked, jogging up lightly beside me. "What's going on?"

"Adam," I said tearfully. "I can't find Gabby…"

He put a firm hand on my shoulder. "Did you tell Sebastian?"

"Yes. He's checking the gift shop."

"Did you tell Mrs. Jameson?"

"No—I don't know—"

"Okay. You keep looking out here. I'll go alert security at the front. They'll call for her over the intercom. We'll find her."

I nodded, trying not to let the motion make the tears spill over and down my cheeks. A plan. Adam had given me a plan, and that made the ground solidify under my feet just a bit, though not quite enough.

"Gabrielle!" I screamed, not worried about how ridiculous

I sounded, as long as Gabby could hear me. By this time, the other Summer Siblings had stood up, wondering at the commotion, including Mrs. Jameson. *Oh, God.* Unable to bear telling her what had happened, I quickly turned away, my eyes darting wildly. I could see Sebastian leaving the gift shop, heading in the same direction Adam had, and still no Gabby...

"Gabrielle Moore!" I called as clearly as I could. "Gabrielle! Gabby!" Her name rang in my ears. Strangers around me were pausing in their paths, looking at me, looking at each other... I started to glare at them, wondering if any of them had touched Gabby... How much time had passed? Two minutes? Twenty?

"Cara?"

Her voice was so soft, almost afraid. I spun around and let out a cry of immense relief, seeing Gabby standing before me on the tiled floor, clutching her starfish pendant. I threw myself down before her and hugged her tightly.

"Gabby, where *were* you?" I asked, pulling away but keeping a tight grip on her shoulders.

Gabby was looking at me like she had never done before, scared and a little wary. "You told me it was a surprise. So I hid so I could surprise you."

"Gabrielle," I said as sternly as I could, though my voice wavered from residual fear and glorious relief. "That was *not* a funny joke. I asked you to go somewhere, and you wandered off without telling me. I thought you went missing, or worse."

"I'm sorry," she said. "It really was just a joke."

"Do not ever do that again, do you understand me?"

"I'm sorry," she repeated. "Are you going to punish me?"

She looked so pitiful, holding on to the star around her

neck, looking up at me with mournful eyes. I touched her cheek gently with my thumb. "No, I'm not going to punish you. I can't do that; I'm not your parent. I just need you to understand how scary this was for me, and I need you to promise you'll never do something like this again."

"I promise," she said. "Can I keep my necklace?"

"Yes, you can keep your necklace," I said, managing a watery smile.

"*Would Gabrielle Moore please report to the front of the aquarium by the entrance lines? Gabrielle Moore, your friends are looking for you! Gabrielle Moore.*"

The intercom system buzzed loudly over the din around us. Gabby looked up towards the ceiling, as if she could find the mysterious source of the voice. "That's me."

"See?" I said. "I was so scared. Everyone's been looking for you."

"I was only gone a minute," she said, curling her lip into a pout.

"That doesn't make it any less scary," I said. "Come on. Let's go up front and show them you're not lost anymore."

My legs felt like jelly as I tried to stand. The other Summer Siblings were gathered in a small semicircle a respectful distance behind us. Mrs. Jameson was making her way over. I pulled Gabby as quickly as I could to the front of the aquarium, holding her hand so tightly that she complained. Both Adam and Sebastian were standing at the entrance with two security guards. Their faces broke into smiles when they saw Gabby. Sebastian turned to the security guards and said something to them. They looked over at me and stepped forward.

"Are you Gabrielle Moore?" one of them asked her. She

nodded and moved closer to me, almost hiding behind my leg.

"And you're Cara Carson?" the other asked me. "Her guardian?"

"I'm Cara," I said. "I'm her guardian for the day, I suppose."

"She's with us," Sebastian said. "The Summer Siblings camp."

"Everything's alright, then?" the second one asked.

"Yes," I confirmed. "She was hiding. As a joke."

"Hiding in a public place like this isn't usually a good joke," the first security guard told Gabby sternly.

"I already gave her the lecture," I said. Both of the guards nodded; one tipped his hat at Gabby, who let out a small giggle. Sebastian shook their hands, then turned to me.

"She's okay?" Adam asked. I walked right up to him and gave him a one-armed hug, not letting go of Gabby's hand. He tensed, then relaxed as he warmly hugged me back.

"Thank you," I said simply.

"Listen, Cara, I'm sorry if I made you mad earlier," he said. "I mean, I kind of meant to, but I'm still sorry about it."

I inhaled, then put it all behind me with one long exhale. "I understand. I really do. So thank you for that, too. I owe you a lot of thanks today."

Adam looked a little puzzled at first, then pleased with himself. "You're welcome."

"But don't get cocky about it," I told him sharply. He laughed.

"I'm really glad Gabby's okay."

"I am, too," I said, looking down at her. She smiled. Mrs. Jameson caught up to us and spoke quietly with Sebastian. My heart revved right back up to its nervous speed.

"Everyone's alright?" she asked Gabby and me. Gabby nodded.

"I'm so, so sorry Mrs. Jameson," I said, Gabby echoing my apology in her thin voice.

"Don't be worried, dear," Mrs. Jameson said. "This sort of thing is bound to happen in a group that has so many children. Let's just all be grateful nothing serious happened."

"I am," I told her quickly. "I'm so, so grateful."

"Listen, Gabby," I said, as we drove back to her house. She was safely buckled in the backseat. "Let's not tell your mom about getting lost at the aquarium."

"I wasn't lost. I was hiding," Gabby said stubbornly. "And that's lying."

"It's not lying," I said. "It's... not telling the whole truth."

"Lying."

"Gabby," I said, glancing at her in the rearview mirror. "I don't want your mom to think I'm irresponsible and that she can't trust me with you. Then she might not let us play together anymore. Do you want that?"

"No," she said, sticking her tongue out a little and staring out the window. I felt a little bad using a scare tactic.

"Okay. So if your mom asks, what are you going to tell her about your day?"

"I'ma tell her that we saw lots and lots of fish and I touched a stingray and then I touched another stingray and then we saw penguins and some more fish and you bought me a necklace," Gabby rattled off.

"It sounds like we had a pretty awesome day," I noted.

"We did!"

"You left out one thing, though."

"What?"

"Reach into my purse on the seat next to you," I told her. She pulled out the plush penguin toy and gasped.

"For me?"

"Yep," I said, grinning and sharing in her delight.

"Thank you, Cara!" Gabby nestled the penguin to her chest and petted its head lovingly. "Now I can tell Momma I got a pet penguin. I love him. I'm gonna name him Cara. Thank you, thank you, thank you!"

"You're welcome," I laughed, pleased at my penguin's namesake. I pulled up in front of her little brick house and told her goodbye. The sun had just barely begun its descent into dusk, still bright, but bringing the chaos of the day to an end. I always felt a little emptier after dropping Gabby off, but today's scare was making the space in my car gape ever wider. I watched her reach the front door, where, to my surprise, she pulled at the handle but had to ring the doorbell. Mrs. Moore came to the door and let her in, then waved at me and held up a finger, indicating that I should wait. I idled in the driveway, wondering what she wanted.

After a minute, she returned to the doorway with Logan balanced on her hip and walked out into the humid heat towards my car. I rolled down my window so we could talk.

"How are you doing, Cara?" she asked. Her eyes still looked as exhausted as they had the first time I had spoken with her, but they were focused.

"Good," I answered, wondering if I should start being anxious. "How are you?"

"I'm good," she said. "Listen, I have a favor to ask of you."

"Sure."

"I've got something of a date tonight… with my husband," she said, and a shy smile broke over her tired face. "We're going to talk things out over dinner."

I wasn't sure how to react, but the odd combination of happiness, nerves, and something like relief reading on her face prompted me to say, "That sounds nice."

"I think so," she said. "I think we're finally ready to try and move forward from all this."

I shifted in my seat, uncomfortable with this excess of information.

"Anyway," Mrs. Moore continued. "My mother will watch Logan for us, but she can't handle both the kids at the same time. A little too much for her at once." She bounced Logan a little as he giggled and wound his fingers into her shirt. "I was hoping you would be able to watch Gabby for us tonight. You don't have to take her out like on one of those camp trips. I would pay you, like a babysitter."

"Oh, no," I said, then quickly elaborated, "I mean, yes, I can watch her, but no, you definitely don't have to pay me."

"You're sure?"

"Of course," I said firmly. "I'd be happy to watch her."

"Thank you," Mrs. Moore said, even more relief lighting her face. "I'm going to be leaving soon to bring Logan to his grandma. You can just stay here, if you want."

I thought for a second, then agreed and went into the house with Mrs. Moore. I had never heard her so talkative. Happiness for Gabby blossomed in me, replacing the weird jealousy and anger I had first felt at the thought of her family coming back together.

"Cara!" Gabby squealed when I came inside.

"Long time, no see," I joked.

"Hey! I just saw you," she protested, ever innocent.

"I'm going to hang out with you tonight," I said. "If that's okay with you."

Gabby nodded happily, then followed her mother to the back bedroom. I stood halfway down the hall in the doorway of Logan's room and watched him stack blocks.

"I'm so grateful for this, Cara," Mrs. Moore called through her closed bedroom door. "There are just too many arguments and dark memories in this house for me and Colin to have a real conversation. Too much hurt."

"I can relate," I called back, thinking of how the door to Aaron's room had stayed shut for years, too painful to open.

"So I think this is going to be good for us. Going out, having dinner, getting to talk. No little girls *hanging on my ankles.*" Gabby burst into a fit of giggles, and I could only imagine that she was clinging to Mrs. Moore's leg.

"We just need a chance," Mrs. Moore continued when I didn't answer. She sounded as if she were trying to convince the two of us that this dinner would be perfect, a magical and effortless solution. What could be easier than eating and talking? "We just need a chance to get back on the right track."

"Of course."

When she finally emerged from her room a few minutes later, she carried herself with confidence. I couldn't help but smile.

"Momma looks beautiful," Gabby informed me solemnly.

"Yes, she does," I agreed. "You really do look fantastic, Mrs. Moore." Her hair was pulled back and tucked into a braided bun, and her maroon colored dress hung spectacularly on her frame. She even had makeup on. I had never seen her like this.

"Thank you again, Cara," she said, hoisting Logan's diaper bag onto her shoulder and shifting her purse into the crook of her arm.

"Momma pick Logan up," Logan burbled. Mrs. Moore smiled and stooped to pluck him up in her free arm.

"I left some money for pizza on the table," she said. "So you can order in if you want. Gabby usually plays outside before bed. You know, running out all that energy. If you go out, take the spare key by the door. Whatever you two wind up doing, just make sure she's in bed before nine," Mrs. Moore said, watching her daughter. "She usually goes to bed earlier, but with you, she'll probably want to stay up. I'm sorry, but I can't give you a time to expect me back. I just don't know."

"That's alright," I assured her. "Take your time. And… good luck."

"Thank you," Mrs. Moore repeated. She crouched as low as she could to give Gabby a kiss, and then I held the door open for her and waved her off.

"Momma looked so pretty," Gabby said, folding her hands under her chin, a goofy smile on her face.

"She sure did," I said. "What would you like to do now, Gabs? I can order pizza, if you want."

"I want to go back to the aquarium."

"Not an option. Try again."

"Run outside!"

"Let's take a walk instead," I suggested. "We'll go around the block a couple times."

"Okay!"

"Go change your shoes," I instructed her, pointing at her sandals.

Gabby scampered off to her room and was back in less than a minute, neither of her sneakers tied, her star pendant bumping against her chest as she ran in tight circles around the living room.

"Remember those chill pills?" I asked, catching her around her waist and bringing her to a halt. "You should take one. And then tie your shoes."

Gabby pantomimed swallowing a pill and gulping down water, after which she obediently bent and looped her laces around into small bows. "Are we really gonna have pizza tonight?"

"Is that what you want?"

"Yes!"

"Then so it shall be!" My imagination tugged at my attention, showing me visions of Gabby surrounded by her loving, attentive parents, both under the same roof, but this time, the picture wasn't clouded by despair on my part. No, I could imagine the Moores wanting date night after date night, and calling me to be their babysitter weekly, if not more often. Long after summer had ended, I'd still have sibling status; I'd still have a purpose. I wanted to call Mrs. Jameson and Ms. Wells right then and there and tell them I had figured it all out. Gabby beamed back up at me.

"Can we go now?"

"Yep." I checked to make sure the knots of her laces were tight. Then I grabbed the spare key, locked the door behind us, and turned left down the block. Gabby shot out ahead of me, beelining for her neighbor's front garden.

"Look at these flowers!" she called. "They're pink!

They're bee-yoo-tee-full!"

"They sure are," I agreed from the sidewalk. "That's called a hibiscus." Gabby stretched her hand out, stroked the papery magenta petals, and then made a sudden movement and snatched the blossom off the plant.

"Gabby!" I cried, disheartened. "You shouldn't have done that."

"It's okay, you can pick flowers."

"But that wasn't your flower to pick. That belonged to your neighbors, and now they can't enjoy it. You really shouldn't take things from other people's yards."

To my surprise, Gabby's eyes filled, her lips trembling. "I'm so sorry!"

I hadn't expected this reaction. "It's okay, Gabby. Now you know."

Gently, ever so gently, she laid the flower on the ground, pulled a patch of mulch over it, and patted it tenderly. "Maybe it will grow back. I'm really, really sorry."

I pressed my hand to my heart. "That was very nice, Gabs. Come on. Next time, just ask me first, okay? We won't take anything that doesn't belong to us, but there might be some things we can have."

Gabby came back to the sidewalk, her head hanging, twisting her fingers together. I put out my arms, and she walked into my hug.

"Let's keep going," I prompted. Gabby sniffled but rebounded quickly. As we walked along, she pointed things out to me, asking permission, getting sillier with each request.

"Can I have this leaf?"

"Yes."

"Can I have this flower?"

"No. It's growing in someone's garden; you know that."

"Can I have this feather?"

"No. Bird diseases."

"Can I have that cloud?"

"Sure, if you can reach it."

"Can I have the sun?"

"No, but you can have the moon, if you want it."

"I want it." We walked on, Gabby collecting pine cones, leaves, pebbles, and the like. Her hands were soon full of her little treasures. She bounced from object to object, inspecting cracks in the sidewalk and running to the curb before I called her back and away from the street.

"Can I have this snail shell?"

"Is there a snail in it?"

She paused. "No."

"Don't lie," I scolded, crouching down and staring in fascination at the slimy, shimmering trail the snail was painting behind itself. "You can't have it if it's a living creature."

"But I want it!"

"Sorry. But the next thing you see, you can have."

We turned a couple of corners, with me being careful to remember the right number of blocks and the order of our turns. I knew that there was a fairly major street nearby, leading to the diner where Mom and I had brought the kids, but we hadn't reached it yet. The sun melted into the canvas of the sky, basking us in what looked like liquid gold and setting fire to the edges of the clouds. I paused, wondering if we should turn back.

"Do we have to go home?" Gabby asked, as if she could read my mind.

I stretched, reaching my fingertips towards the glory above me and looked down at Gabby. She laid down her collection item by item, a neat row of leaves, pine cones, fallen flower petals, and sticks.

"Look. I'll leave everything here if we can go just a little more!"

"Okay," I agreed, not ready myself to end what had turned out to be, overall, an excellent day. I could see something like a future for myself. Exactly what it was, I wasn't quite sure, but it made me feel light. "Let's go a couple more blocks. But after that, we have to turn back and head home for dinner."

"And I can have the next thing I see? You promised."

"Sure, if it meets all the rules."

Gabby beamed and took off running down the street, turning the corner sharply. I jogged after her, barely able to hear her voice calling back to me over the sudden increase of traffic sounds.

"This way!"

I rounded the corner, saw Gabby, reached out for her as she pointed to something just beyond the curb, glinting in the light.

"Oooh! A penny!"

"Gabby—"

"You said I could have it!"

"No!"

Gabby stretched out her little hand, lost her balance, stutter-stepped into the street—

And then it happened.

CHAPTER 14

Who was to blame? Myself? The driver? Gabby?

All I was aware of was the burning in my ankle and the uncomfortable angles of my own body. Pain flashed red behind my eyelids.

I slowly opened my eyes, confused, afraid. I still couldn't see anything. Shaking, I tried to raise my head, but my neck resisted. My hip, my whole side, throbbed, dull and steady. I ached.

And just like that, I knew where I was, and what had happened, like an electric shock had jolted me into the sudden knowledge. *No no no.* Despite my body's resistance, I pulled my head up and extracted my arms from underneath the weight that was holding them down.

Sounds pressed against my eardrums, garbled, frantic, shrill. Slowly, the sounds separated themselves into distinguishable words.

"Are you okay?"

"Can you hear me?"

"Are you okay?"

"Are you okay?"

"Miss, are you okay?"

A wail was tearing itself from my mouth. She was in my lap. I didn't know how I had gotten to her, but there she was, cradled in my arms. Her right temple was scraped, bleeding; there was gravel in the wound; she was unconscious.

My mouth was trying to form her name, but my teeth were chattering, smashing against each other. My shoulders were shaking uncontrollably; my fingers were trembling; someone was trying to pull me away from Gabby, but I curled myself over her again, refusing to let them move me.

"Somebody call an ambulance. Somebody call 9-1-1."

I sobbed.

"Are you okay?"

I was tired of hearing that, I was tired of the noise, I was tired. I couldn't understand how my heart could be beating so quickly, fighting to break free of my chest, while my eyes just wanted to close and carry me to sleep at the same time.

Sirens shrieked. My tongue pushed a single word through.

"No, no, no, no, no…"

"She won't answer me."

"Someone's got to get her off that little girl."

"No, don't move her. What if they're hurt?"

"Look at her ankle."

A new voice: "Everyone move back, please."

Hands were on me, strong and deft, peeling me carefully off of Gabby, pressing all over me, on my hip, on my ankle, hovering there as I yelped.

"Take a deep breath," said the clear and commanding voice near my head. "You're okay. Can you move your arms, your legs?"

I tried to do as they instructed, allowing a shuddering breath to fill my lungs, my eyes fixed on Gabby all the while. A paramedic was lifting her eyelids and shining a penlight at her face.

"What's your name?"

"Cara Carson."

"Cara. I'm Dave. You're going to be fine," my paramedic told me. "Do you feel any numbness?"

I took stock of my limbs, then shook my head.

"We're going to lift you onto this stretcher," said Dave. "On three."

I didn't fight, didn't speak, only kept my eyes on Gabby. Inside the ambulance, I ignored the hands as they hooked me up to their monitors, making no protestations, only straining to see Gabby lying on her stretcher outside. A second ambulance waited for her with its back doors open, a mirror-image of the one I was in.

"I'm going to splint your ankle for you," Dave said. "It looks broken. We'll get a cold pack on it that will keep the swelling down."

I still didn't say anything, just let him work on my ankle while I focused on Gabby, who was still outside. Her paramedic was carefully strapping a sturdy collar around her neck. Dave followed my gaze.

"Do you know her?" he asked.

"That's Gabby," I said, the only thing I could say. He understood. Taking pity on me, he climbed out of the ambulance. "I'll check on her for you. Hang tight."

"Gabby," I called again after him. Dave spoke quickly with Gabby's paramedic while helping him move her stretcher into her own ambulance. My heart slammed itself against my chest as Dave headed back towards me, Gabby's ambulance speeding off.

"Please," I choked out. "Please tell me— is she okay?"

"She'll need a CT scan at the hospital," he said.

I didn't understand, but I nodded, thirsty for information.

"You got yourself between her and the car?"

I nodded again. Dave looked at me thoughtfully but didn't say anything, turning instead to check on my ankle. I closed my eyes, wondering if Ms. Wells would give me a pass, just this once, to not be present, to mentally check out, to not have to remember what happened the last time my sibling was in an ambulance.

They made me stay overnight at the hospital, to observe me, maybe to see if the guilt would physically manifest as it tried to consume me. They set my broken ankle straight and explained the severity of the bruising on my hip and side, where the car made full contact, then drugged me up. But as it wore off, the guilt crept in and took its place.

I had failed Mrs. Moore, who had left her beloved daughter in my care while she tried to repair her relationship with her husband. I had failed my mother, whose face had crumpled into utter, unspeakable agony when she saw her last child folded and shaking in a hospital bed. I had failed Mrs. Jameson, who had trusted me and let me into the Summer Siblings on the expectation that I would do no harm to my sibling, and I had failed Ms. Wells, who had believed I could handle this responsibility. And worst, worst of all, I had failed Gabby, beyond words, beyond forgiveness.

Mom, blessedly, didn't make me talk. I had expected a barrage of questions, but none came. She held my hand, stroked my hair, examined the colors of my deepening bruises. I supposed the doctors had explained and told her all she needed to know. I tried to read her face to see if she knew what was happening to Gabby, stealing glances when she thought I wasn't looking, but if she knew, she wasn't revealing anything. As much as I wanted to, I knew better than to ask to see Gabby. I didn't deserve it.

When I was eventually discharged and had hobbled on my crutches to the car, Mom finally asked her first question.

"What now, Cara, sweetie?" Her worn, exhausted face was lined in sympathy for me. "What do you want to do now?"

I knew what I wanted but didn't deserve. I thought, and then asked for something I had never willingly asked for before.

"Can I see Ms. Wells?"

The first thing Ms. Wells did when I limped into her office the next day was to pull me into a long, tight hug. I stood helplessly caught in her embrace. She guided me to the sofa and sat me down. I leaned my crutches against the arm of the sofa, not sure of what I wanted to say or ask. Thankfully, Ms.

Wells spoke first.

"She's okay, Cara. Gabby's okay."

My breath caught. I dropped my head in relief, in exhaustion, in gratitude. Tears leaked down from the corners of my eyes. I was so tired of crying, but I couldn't hold it back.

"She is?"

"Yes. In fact, I have permission from her parents to tell you everything, if you want to hear it," she said, showing me a scrap of paper with notes scribbled all over it. "Your mom called me, and I called Earla, and she called the Moores, and, well, we've all been speaking. The doctors were concerned about Gabby having a head bleed, which is why she needed the scan, but it came out fine. She had a very mild concussion from when she hit her head on the concrete, and she was a little confused at first, but she's just fine now."

"I knocked her over," I interrupted. The words jammed in my throat, bottlenecked, and then the dam broke. "I ran to her to try to protect her, but I pushed her over, but I swear, it was an accident—"

"Cara," Ms. Wells said, in the firmest voice she'd ever used with me. "You need to understand that if you hadn't been there, if you hadn't put yourself between the car and Gabby, Gabby would be in a much, much worse situation than she is now."

I shuddered.

"Mrs. Moore said Gabby's been asking for you," Ms. Wells continued. "But they wanted to wait to get her home and settled before letting her see you again. Apparently, she's very easily excited."

She smiled at me, but I wasn't ready to smile back.

"This is all good news, Cara. Gabby's fine. They patched

up the scrape on her head, and she's going home today. She has a little bruising, and she might wind up with a small scar, but overall, she's perfectly fine. You saved her, Cara. You really did."

"But..." I could feel my throat closing. "But she wouldn't have gotten hurt if she hadn't been out on the walk with me. This wouldn't have happened if I hadn't..."

"Stop right there, Cara," Ms. Wells said. "We've talked about this before. You're bordering on spiral thinking. This is a useless, hopeless game to play with yourself. It's not fair to you. It's not fair to anyone."

"I can't help it."

"Yes, you can."

I hunched over, pressing my forehead to my knees as the avalanche of guilt swept over me again. "I can't make it stop. I keep replaying everything in my head. I see Gabby stumbling, and then I see the car coming straight at her— and then all I see is the blood on her head and the medics strapping her down."

"I think it might help if you see her in person," Ms. Wells suggested. "If you give the Moores another day or so, I'm sure you can call them and ask to see Gabby."

"I know what they're going to say. Mrs. Moore's going to tell me how grateful she is that I was there, or something like that. She's going to think I'm the reason Gabby is okay, but I'm really the reason she got hurt. I used Gabby. I was selfish. I needed her, and all I did in return was get her hurt."

Ms. Wells didn't respond immediately. She folded her hands in her lap, on top of the folder with her notes, and gave me a long look.

"Tell me how all this makes you feel."

"Guilty!"

"Beyond that."

"I'm miserable. Upset. I can't believe this happened. Everything was going so great, and then *this*."

"Everything was going so great," Ms. Wells repeated. She opened my file and flipped through the pages without looking at them. "That's the most positive thing I've heard you say in the past three years."

I frowned.

"You know what emotion I'm sensing the most from you, Cara?"

"Frustration?" I snapped.

"Love," Ms. Wells said quietly. "All of your anger, frustration, and guilt stems from love."

"Seems a pretty crappy deal to me."

"To me, it proves that your previous experiences have not robbed you of your ability to love. They haven't ruined your ability to see good in the world. They haven't stolen your passion. And that's a good thing."

I looked at Ms. Wells, completely speechless at how she had found something positive in the rubble.

"This is good, Cara."

"I know," I mumbled, surprising myself. "I know."

"Wait another day, and then give Mrs. Moore a call," she said gently. "See Gabby. And then we can keep moving forward from here. This is a small moment in the longevity of life. We just have to push on."

I barely made it through the next twenty-four hours, waiting to call Mrs. Moore. When I finally felt like an appropriate amount of time had passed, I dialed the Moores' number and pressed the phone to my ear impatiently.

"Mrs. Moore? It's Cara," I said, holding my breath.

"Oh, my goodness," she said. "Cara!"

"Mrs. Moore, I'm so, so, so sorry," I began in a rush, my prepared apology lost in my distress. "I'm so sorry, I can't even begin to tell you how awful I feel."

"Oh, Cara, no, please don't apologize," she said, and then, as expected: "We're so glad you were there. You really saved Gabby."

Ms. Wells had coached me on how to respond to this; even if I felt I didn't deserve the gratitude, I needed to be mindful of Mrs. Moore's feelings and respect them. I didn't argue. "I just did it without thinking. I had to help Gabby."

"You're an angel."

"Mrs. Moore, I was really calling to ask if… if I could come see Gabby."

There was just the slightest pause on the other end of the line. "Of course. Tomorrow?"

To wait another day would be torture, but I had no choice. "Tomorrow. See you then."

By the next day, all of my emotions seemed to be fighting within me for top billing. Excitement, anxiety, guilt, and other unidentifiable feelings filtered through me, filling me to the brim with confusion and resulting in a stomachache. I stood on the Moores' doorstep and waited for someone to let me in, very much aware of the blue car in the driveway.

When Mrs. Moore finally welcomed me in, I couldn't help but read something on her face that troubled me. I just couldn't quite place what it was. My insides knotted themselves even more tightly.

"How's Gabby?" I asked quickly.

"Milking this for all it's worth," Mrs. Moore smiled. "She's such a ham. You can go down to her room; she's in her bed. The doctor said we should keep her calm and well-rested for a couple of days, take it easy, but it's been hard with all this extra attention. She's loving it."

I didn't look around for Mr. Moore, instead going straight down the hall to Gabby's room. She was lying with one leg dangling off her bed, the other hidden by the rumpled pink blankets, and she was clutching Giraffe as well as a doll, whispering to them conspiratorially. She was whole.

"Hey, Gabs," I said. She looked up with purest joy shining from her face.

"Cara!" she squealed, then immediately clasped a hand over her mouth. "I'm supposed to use my inside voice."

"Yeah, you are," I said, awkwardly lowering myself to the floor beside her bed and stretching my leg with the cast out in front of me. Her bed was low enough so that we were almost on the same level. "How are you feeling?"

"Dizzy!" she said, flinging herself backwards on the bed and throwing an arm across her forehead. "I need more soda!"

I glanced at the half-full glass on her little nightstand. "I think you have enough."

She giggled. "Momma usually doesn't let me have soda. She's been making me drink a lot of water, but today she let me have a Coke!"

I stared at the huge bandage on her temple, wondering how badly it would scar. When she turned her head away from me, she looked like her usual self. I reached out and took her small brown hand in mine.

"Gabby, I just really want to say that I'm sorry," I said,

willing myself not to cry in front of her. "I can't believe this happened to you."

I bit my lip, the desire to claim the incident as my fault pushing forward, but Ms. Wells had declared so many times that it was an untruth that I wasn't sure if I should say it.

"It's okay, Cara," Gabby said, patting my hand. "You saved me from that car!"

"I really didn't," I said. "I need you to understand that... well, I need us both to understand that even though it was a freak accident, I didn't save you."

She looked at me.

"I didn't cause it, but I didn't save you," I said, but it didn't sound quite right. Telling her that she really saved me sounded too cheesy, too happy-ending. Her fingers wiggled against mine. I couldn't think of anything else to say.

"Can I sign your cast?" she asked, as if the previous conversation hadn't even happened.

"This isn't the kind of cast you sign," I explained, drawing my leg towards me and showing her my foot. "It's more like a boot."

"Can I sign something?"

"Uh..." I looked at my clothes. "I guess you can write your name on my hand."

"On your face?"

"On my *hand*."

Gabby glanced at the door, then ran across the room and grabbed a marker from a box in her closet. "Don't tell Momma I was out of bed." She took my extended hand, the back of which I presented to her, and flipped it over, carefully writing her name on my palm.

"There. Now it's kind of like I'm holding your hand even

when I'm not!" she said excitedly. "Look, close your hand. I'm in it!"

"Very cool," I said. She cuddled Giraffe under her neck and fiddled with the doll's dark hair. "Tell me about your doll."

She gave me Giraffe to hold while she showed me her doll, and we chatted for a while about her toys until Mrs. Moore tapped on Gabby's door.

"Let's try to take a nap, Gabrielle," she said. "Did she leave her bed, Cara?"

"Nope," I said, winking at Gabby. "She's been a perfect patient."

Mrs. Moore smiled and took the soda from the nightstand, then helped me stand. "I hope you didn't drink too much sugar to keep you from settling down."

"I hate naps," Gabby complained. "I'm not even a little tired."

"Giraffe's tired," Mrs. Moore said, scooping the stuffed animal off the floor and tucking it in next to Gabby. "He needs a sleepy buddy."

Gabby burrowed under the covers, hiding her face.

"Tell Cara goodbye," said Mrs. Moore. "You can talk with her more later. I'll even bring the phone in here, and you can call her the second you wake up."

"I'd like that," I chimed in. "Get some rest, Gabby."

"Okay," she said, her voice muffled by the blankets. Mrs. Moore turned off the light, then ushered me out of the room and into the hall.

"Cara, if you have a few minutes, Colin and I would like to talk to you before you go," she said, the same odd expression from earlier blanketing her face. My heart dropped. I followed her to the kitchen, where Mr. Moore was sitting at the table. I must have looked nervous, because he quickly smiled and pulled out a chair for me.

"Hello," he said warmly. I was struck by how different his tone was. I pressed my hands together in my lap and looked blankly at the two people sitting before me.

"First of all, I think we both wanted an opportunity to thank you face-to-face," he said. I opened my mouth to protest, but Mrs. Moore smiled and held up her hand to stop me.

"I told him you wouldn't accept our thanks," she said. "But we truly do have so much to thank you for. For saving Gabby from that car and for being a light for her during this dark time."

"You have to understand how complicated all this was for us," Mr. Moore said. "We appreciate the role you played in our daughter's life in the middle of it all."

It was no use telling them that the real thanks should go to Mrs. Jameson, to Ms. Wells, to my mom, to themselves. I didn't dare breathe. I knew this wasn't all they wanted to talk to me about. They glanced at each other, and finally, Mrs. Moore let the smile fall from her face.

"Cara, with everything that's been going on recently, we had to make a decision on how to best move forward as a family," she said, holding my gaze. I looked straight through her eyes, unseeing. "And we've talked it over, and we feel the best thing for us to do right now is to leave this place behind us. We're going to be moving."

When I didn't say anything, Mr. Moore leaned forward. "My mother lives in Ohio, and she knows someone there who's willing to rent their house to us until we can find somewhere more permanent. We've looked at it from every angle, and this is what makes sense for us."

I didn't move.

"We know how close you and Gabby are, which is why we wanted to tell you immediately," Mrs. Moore said. She took a breath. "For once, everything's been falling into place for us. We're leaving in three weeks. We want to get Gabby up there and settled before the school year starts."

What hurt more, getting hit by the car, or this?

"Gabby doesn't know yet. We're going to tell her tonight," Mrs. Moore continued. "We just wanted to let you know. I'm so sorry, Cara. Gabby loves you so much, and we're so grateful to you for so many things. We just have to do what we think is best for our family."

"I understand," I said, expressionless.

"Are you okay?" Mrs. Moore asked. She looked concerned. "Can I get you something to drink?"

"I'm fine," I said, shaking myself mentally and forcing my expression into what I hoped was a polite smile. "Thank you for telling me. I have to go, though."

"Cara, I know this must be terribly hard for you to hear," started Mrs. Moore. Mr. Moore looked from his wife to me and back again.

"No, you're right, you have to do what's best. I really have to go," I said, fumbling with my crutches and half-hopping to the door.

"Cara?"

"You have to move forward," I said, echoing both Mrs. Moore and Ms. Wells, the phrase stale in my mouth.

"I know you must be hurting—"

"Um, can you tell Gabby maybe not to call me when she

wakes up? I'll call her tomorrow," I said, and without waiting for an answer, I left.

CHAPTER 15

Audie Wells was sympathetic but encouraging, her default setting. At my next appointment with her, which Mom had set up, I almost detected a flash of despondency for me, which she tried to hide. Was she as acutely aware of how much progress I had made that was now gone? I cut her off before she could utter a single word about moving forward and limped from the office without saying anything when our hour was up.

Mom let me cry for a good long while but was soon trying to distract me daily, taking me shopping, bringing me new books, recording shows and insisting I watch with her. Once she started to mention signing me up for a national sibling program, but she stopped when she saw my face.

The news somehow made it through to the rest of the Summer Siblings. Some of them, like Julie, texted me, expressing how bad they felt for me. Adam sent me multiple texts, paragraphs, even called me once, but I didn't answer. I never heard from Chase. Isa, to my surprise, kindly invited me to hang out with her and her sister Nina. I thanked her, but declined.

Mrs. Jameson was the only one who didn't offer any advice or distractions. Mrs. Moore had pulled Gabby from the camp before we were finished with our events, keeping the family close, packing up and rebuilding their bonds. When I went to Mrs. Jameson's office to do the mandatory exit interview from the program, she asked if there was anything I wanted to talk about. We sat in silence for a solid five minutes, and then she put her hand on mine when I still couldn't say anything. She pulled me up from my chair into a close hug, and then let me leave without saying another word. She kissed the top of my head, patted my cheek, and physically turned me around towards the door, handing me my crutches and sending me away. It wasn't much, but it was enough.

My last day with Gabby was two days before her family left. We were at our favorite place, Pop's Ice Cream Parlor, enjoying one last scoop.

"I'm moving," Gabby told the girl behind the counter. "This is the last time I can get ice cream with my big sister."

"Then this treat's on the house," the girl said, waving my money away. Gratitude swept through me.

"Thank you—" I started, but realized I didn't know her name. I glanced at the tag on her apron. "Lisa. Really. Thank you, Lisa."

We sat inside this time, basking in the air conditioning. Neither of us talked much. Gabby had never been this quiet.

"I'll write to you every single day," she finally said.

I smiled, but I knew how unrealistic the claim was. "I'll write back every single time."

"Am I gonna like my new school?"

"Yes."

"Am I gonna like my new room?"

"Yes."

She poked at her ice cream. "Am I gonna have another big sister?"

I paused. "I don't know. There might be another program or buddy system at your new school."

"Just like the Summer Siblings?"

"Maybe." I imagined her bonding with someone else in the same way we had, and took a deep breath, and gave her the advice I had never followed for myself. "But Gabby, if there is, and if you're able to, you should do it."

"I should?"

"Yes. You should meet as many new people as possible and do everything you can," I said quickly, fighting for the words, feeling like I had to say everything I could while I still had the time. "Don't let your life stop just because you're worried or scared. Do and try everything you can."

"Cara?"

"Yeah?"

"I'm gonna miss you *so much*," she said, slipping out of her chair and clinging to my side. I pressed my face against the cloud of her hair and hugged her back.

"Your ice cream's melting," I said after a minute.

"I don't want it anymore. I don't wanna go."

"Yes, you do," I said. "You and your mom and dad and Logan are going to get to start all over. Your mom told me you're going to have a whole room to yourself without any of the baby's things in it. You're going to get to hang out with your grandma all the time. You're going to make new friends.

You're going to have so much fun. And you'll hear from me all the time. Until you're all grown up, and even then, you'll still hear from me."

She didn't say anything. An idea came to me.

"Here," I said, reaching into my purse and hiding something in my hand. "A little present for you."

She still looked crestfallen, but her eyes focused on my hand. I took her index finger and slid the leather clasp of my penny keychain onto it.

"This belonged to my brother, Aaron," I said. "Whenever I miss him, I hold onto it. See how it has a star shape in the middle? I press it on my skin and look at the star and think about him."

"I can keep it?" she asked.

"Yes. It matches your starfish necklace."

"Thank you, Cara," she said, pressing the penny against her palm and gazing at the star. "I'm going to keep this forever!"

I sat back, heartbroken but happy, watching her play with Aaron's keychain. She slurped at her melted ice cream but soon pushed it away, engrossed in the star on her skin. I wiped down our table and tossed our napkins and cups into the trash.

"Say thank you again," I told Gabby, pointing at Lisa, who waved at us.

"Thank you," Gabby said to the girl. Then she turned to me and hugged my leg. "Thank you."

I knelt down and hugged her back. "Thank *you*."

The last Summer Siblings event of the season, a big kickball tournament, took place a week after Gabby's family moved. I hadn't planned to do so, but I found myself driving out to it, to the same park where the first general play day event had been. I felt like a moth irresistibly pulled toward a light, drawn and fixated, though there was nothing to benefit me.

Everyone was there, teenagers and kids and counselors, Mrs. Jameson enjoying it all from the shade of a huge umbrella. I didn't want her to notice me, not after we had shared our quiet moment at the exit interview, so I watched from afar, leaning against a tree and trying not to think about how Gabby and I should have been out there.

The ball rolled my way a couple of times, but I wasn't familiar with any of the campers who came to retrieve it. If I were waiting for a magical moment to address anyone, I would have to make it happen myself.

I watched Sebastian mingling with the other counselors, positioning himself near Ms. Wells whenever he could. I had to admit that their obvious differences made the thought of them together all the sweeter. I decided I didn't have to talk to either of them right now. Sebastian's path may not ever cross with mine again, but I knew Ms. Wells' would. I still had more things to figure out and talk through. When I was ready, I would call her.

Isa was easy to pick out among the crowd, clapping and directing people on her team like she was captain. Julie was on the opposite team, laughing and chatting, perfectly cool and casual. Once, I thought she might have spotted me and waved, but she just as easily could have been trying to get someone else's attention, and I didn't wave back. I had both Isa's and Julie's numbers if I ever wanted to pursue better friendships. I was surprised by how comforting that thought was. I knew Julie would happily pick up our friendship right where it had left off three years ago. Isa might take some getting used to, but I could probably learn from her.

There was only one person I was relatively interested in talking to today. I had to search for him but spotted him soon enough, hanging around the water table full of little cups. I slowly made my way towards him, keeping a safe distance, wondering how to get his attention.

"Chase!" I called once I was behind him, still a good twenty feet back. *"Chase!"*

It took several attempts, as I was trying not to raise my voice too much, before he finally looked over his shoulder and spotted me. I waved him over, away from the group.

"Why are you hiding all the way out here?" he asked.

"Well, Gabby isn't here."

"So?"

"So... I mean... it's just kind of weird and uncomfortable," I said. "You heard what happened with Gabby, right?"

"Yeah."

He didn't ask or comment about the situation, just dropped the single word and waited for me to continue. I tried to remember what it was about him that had ever seemed remotely attractive.

"Chase, can I ask you a question?"

"Yeah."

"Why aren't you going to college?"

Chase blinked, almost in surprise. "I don't want to. There's no law that says you *have* to go to college."

"I know, but what are you planning to do instead? Like, trade school? Work for a family business? I don't know, travel or something?"

"What's the big deal?" Chase asked. "I'll figure something out, I guess."

"What do your parents think?"

Chase laughed. "I live with my mom. She's happy to have me home as long as I want to stay."

I was suddenly and immensely grateful to my mom, who, despite never insisting I go to college, had only allowed me two weeks of pointless wallowing before prodding me into action with Ms. Wells.

"Why do you care?" Chase asked.

"I was just curious, I guess," I said. Deep down, I think I had hoped that there had been a really good reason, something that would make me understand, but I realized that I wasn't surprised. "You should get back to the kickball game."

"Hey," he said, even though he was already walking back to the water table. He flashed me a quick smile. "Remember that coffee shop I saw you at? Want to meet me back there one day?"

"Thanks," I said, "but no." He shrugged and ambled the rest of the way to the field. I turned our conversation over and over again in my mind, thinking, deciding. As it turned out, there was actually one other person I wanted to talk to here.

The fourth anniversary of Aaron's death loomed less than a month away. The Louisiana heat lingered, no hint of an upcoming autumn.

Gabby hadn't quite kept her promise of daily letters, not that I had expected her to. In the month that she had been

gone, she had written me about ten times. I constantly wanted
to send her things but didn't want to force anything on her as
she started her new life, so I held myself to only responding to
what she sent me. She also called me about once a week, just
to chat. The calls were sporadic and didn't follow any sort of
schedule, causing me to jump in anticipation every time my
phone rang.

But her letters were the real comfort to me, as I hoped
mine were for her. Hers mostly consisted of pictures she drew
and small words that she printed. Often, one of her parents
wrote what she apparently dictated. I tried to make mine
short and easy to read, forcing my handwriting into large and
even letters. Occasionally I included a small pen doodle for
her amusement. I thought often about the Summer Siblings'
final letter, in which I was supposed to impart wisdom and
advice. I never wrote it, because I had no intention of there
being any finality in my correspondence with Gabby.

I felt just as much comfort in sending her a letter as I did
in receiving them. That's when the idea came to me.

The only time I had been to Aaron's grave was his
funeral. I hadn't been able to bear even the thought of Aaron
in his close-quartered box, bones and dust beneath my feet, let
alone go and face it in person. But it was time for that to
change.

I briefly thought about simply leaving my letter at his
grave, to let the wind carry it wherever it wanted to go, but I
didn't like the idea of somebody finding and reading what was
meant only for my brother. So I took some calming breaths
and approached his grave with the intention to stay, settling
in the soft grass by the hot stone on which his name was
inscribed.

"I wrote you a letter, Aaron," I whispered. A crow cawed over my head. I stretched a little, feeling awkward, like I was being watched. I had not talked to him out loud in years. I drew a shaky breath and looked down at the stone, then up at the sky, then out in the distance. "I'm... I'm going to read it to you, okay? I guess it's silly of me to ask. Alright. Okay." I forced myself to stop, to take a deep breath. "I'm just... I'm just gonna start."

What was I so nervous about? The too-green cover of Ms. Wells' notebook dazzled against the natural green of the grass. I flipped through the pages of journaling until I reached my last and latest entry. I exhaled deeply and finally began to read from the page, quietly.

"Dear Aaron. I miss you so much. That sentence is too simple to explain how badly, how deeply I miss you. I miss you in the quiet moments when I can see the space between the stars in the sky. I miss you in the face of the blinding sunrise, the ones I watch from my window when I can't sleep. The ones that bring a new dawn, a new day, reminding me that life goes on for me, that I have new beginnings to make, even though it's not the same for you. I wonder if you get sunrises and sunsets wherever you are. If you do, I hope they're beautiful.

"I miss your voice when the wind whistles in my ears and presses against my eardrums, making a sound that I can't quite describe. Sometimes I feel like I'm forgetting what you sound like. I miss your embrace and reassuring grip whenever I'm nervous or upset. I wish you could hug me now."

My body ached for a hug, for physical contact from someone, anyone. I lay down in the grass, settling against the sturdiness, the physicality of the ground. Something sharp dug into my back, but I ignored it and held the letter over my head, continuing to read, my voice louder, stronger. "I miss you in my bones and in my blood and in my love. I miss you so deeply that no matter how much or what I eat, this indefinable hunger will never be satiated. I miss you infinitely. I miss you steadily. I miss you with all that I am and all that I do. I miss you so much it hurts me, like a disease or illness that doctors can't diagnose. It hurts so much that sometimes, I'm just numb.

"I miss you. I have accepted that. But I've seen how other people deal with missing their own loved ones, and I didn't know this before, but I know it now. Even though I will never stop missing you, I will be okay. Even though it's been almost four years, I guess I'm not over the shock of us not growing up together, of having to learn things on my own, of not being protected by you. But maybe you're still protecting me. I'll never know if the things that happen to me are coincidences or acts of providence guided by you. But I've learned that the joy and mystery of life is part of accepting this not knowing.

"I have to trust that the pain will subside. If I'm honest with myself, some of it already has; I just wasn't sure how to register that, or if that was okay to happen. I have a beautiful little sister named Gabby. You would love her. She would love you. She's the reason I'm writing to you right now. I can practically hear her telling me to say hi to you from her. I'm sure Mom would want to say hi, too, although I guess she could do that on her own. Sorry for rambling. Sorry for apologizing.

"I miss you, Aaron. I love you. But I can't stop time from carrying me forward, and I can't stop life, and I don't want to. I will never stop missing you, and I will never stop loving you, and I want you to know that. And I want you to know that I'm going to be alright. I want myself to know that I'll be alright."

The breeze carried my voice up and away from me, dissolving the words into mere sounds, dissolving sounds into nothingness. Some of what I had said had been written; some spilled from me unprompted. I thought that I could have lay there in front of the grave forever, but that was not a productive way to spend a life. Besides, something was still trying to poke its way through my back. I rolled over and sat up, then, curious, turned back around and started feeling through the blades of grass, looking for a rock or shell. My fingertips finally closed around something small and hard, which I pulled from the soft dirt.

A penny. A completely whole, somewhat dirty, not very shiny, dingy penny. The dull metal was lackluster as could be between my fingers, but I still felt a thrill shoot up my spine. I looked to the sky, where the bright sun and puffy clouds hung, answerless, but complete.

"Alright," I said. "I get it. I understand."

And I did understand. I finally understood that my life, however much was left of it, days or years or decades, would be an enormous jumble of not understanding. And being able to accept that was enough, paradoxically enough.

I tore the pages out of the notebook and tucked the letter into my pocket with the intention to destroy it when I got home. It had done its part. With penny in hand, I stood, brushed the dirt off the backs of my legs, and walked steadily out of the cemetery, my face dry and eyes clear. At my car, I stopped and dropped the penny to the ground, watching it roll and finally settle several yards away on the asphalt.

Someone else could have it. No lucky penny or keychain or fortune cookie could give me a luck that didn't exist; I had to create my own paths. And the first path I had created would lead me to my meeting next week with the local community college advisor to talk about some options. Maybe a degree in social work. Maybe not. I thought of what Mom would say when she found out I set up this meeting on my own. I thought of what Ms. Wells might say at our next appointment. I thought of what Adam would say when I told him at our date this afternoon, having agreed to keep in touch after the Summer Siblings kickball tournament. It would be our fourth date in as many weeks.

I thought of what Aaron would think, but for once, I didn't dwell on it. I was proud to be his sister, but I didn't have to let that be my only definition.

My phone buzzed in my pocket. I pulled it out quickly and saw Gabby's name lighting up the screen. I hesitated, then put it back in my pocket, with the promise to call her as soon as I got home. For now, I simply wanted to enjoy this moment in the light, with my face turned to the sun and my feet firmly on the ground. A smile pulled at my lips, and without the smallest sense of doubt, I knew, *I knew*, that Aaron's death wasn't the end. Gabby's leaving wasn't the end. It all hurt, but here I was, my breathing body proof that nothing that had happened so far was the end.

I couldn't see where the path led beyond my meeting next week, but I knew that it didn't matter. No more stopping, no more going in circles, no more waiting. I just had to keep moving forward.

ACKNOWLEDGMENTS

Like good stewards of the manifold grace of God, serve one another with whatever gift each of you has received. 1 Peter 4:10

The reality of this book is due in large part to the patient and loving people in my life who walked with me on this journey.

I owe a lifetime of gratitude to my parents, Rick and Angela, who ingrained in me the idea that I could do anything I put my mind to, as long as I was willing to work for it. Your love for our family has been an anchor in my life, and I am proud to be your daughter. (Special thanks to my mom for being the first person to ever read a draft of this book and for crying in all the right places.)

Thank you to my husband, Michael, who treated the idea of me writing a book as a certainty, not just a dream, right from the start. Thank you for reading the entire manuscript out loud to me so I could hear it in a different way. Thank you for all of your technical help in formatting and publishing. ("You have much knowledge.") Thank you for every sacrifice you make for our family so that I could have the time and resources to accomplish goals like this. Thank you for loving me in the unconditional way that you do.

I'm deeply grateful for both the edits and companionship of Erin Classen, who has stuck by my side not just for the duration of this novel, but for over a decade of friendship. Your gentle critiques and confidence in my words have made this book better and brought me peace. It would not be the same novel without your notes, corrections, and love.

My sister, Alyssa, has been the source of more laughter and conspiracy theories than a regular sibling relationship should have, and I'm so proud to be your friend. You inspire me so immensely with your life. Whether you realize it or not, you have taught me so much about being a sister, which was crucial to writing this book.

Thank you to Julie Vaughn for your graphic design prowess that resulted in the beautiful cover design. Your talent in turning the abstract into a reality truly gave this book a "face," so to speak!

Although this book existed in draft form before my son did, I found myself rewriting certain parts after becoming a mother and gaining insight into an incalculably deeper world of love. Benjamin An, you have brought me so much more joy than I could put into words. I hope you know that, just as my parents taught me, you can do whatever you set your mind to. Finishing this book has proved to me that I can be a mother and a person of my own at the same time, and hopefully a person you can be proud of. I love you so much, little boy.

Finally, like so very many authors before me, I want to thank you, the reader, for giving this book a chance. It has existed in my head for so long that it's nearly overwhelming to know that it now exists as part of you. I hope you have enjoyed reading it as much as I enjoyed writing it.

ABOUT THE AUTHOR

Erica Kelly Tran was born and raised just outside of New Orleans, LA, where she continues to live with her husband and son. She works as an administrative assistant for a Catholic retreat movement and has previously worked in advertising as a copy and ghostwriter. Beyond writing blogs for other people, she currently has exactly zero writing credentials, publications, or awards, so please take her cheeky word for it when she simply says that she loves to write.